DRAGONS OF
WENDAL

Maria E. Schneider

Bear Mountain Books

Dragons of Wendal
Maria E. Schneider
Copyright June 2012 © Maria E. Schneider

Printing History: POD printing July 2012
E-format 2012

Cover Art:
Assnezana (cover background): http://www.facebook.com/assnezana
Character and clothing: http://www.folkvangar.com/store/
Crystal: DepositPhotos/Jetz
Dragon: DepositPhotos/Gurbi4

ISBN-13: 978-0615657585 (Bear Mountain Books)
ISBN-10: 0615657583

Acknowledgments

Big thanks to Lindis for letting me name a character after her; it fits so perfectly! I suspect she is much nicer and possibly shorter than the book character, but no less an honorable warrior. To all my fans who write and ask for more stories, thank you. And thanks to all the writers who toil away, creating stories that inspire me, make me smile and entertain. A special and hearty thanks to my beta readers: April, my dragon expert; Michelle Scott, who has penned more than a few magical adventures of her own; and Cinderspark, who flings fairy dust with abandon, helping the magic along. And I would not be who I am today if not for my husband who helps make my dreams come true.

DRAGONS OF WENDAL

Prologue – Snitched, Snatched

Cousin Lonnie was a complete idiot.

I stormed through the castle gates, barely slowing to let Trevor register that it was just me, "helpful little Zoe." Some of the other guards hassled women on principle and me out of spite. To some degree they all suspected I was a wizard, but like their king, most of them refused to believe a woman could be powerful enough to be dangerous.

Lonnie, like the wizard before him, was stationed at the top of the castle, which meant too many stairs. I took them two at a time, hugging the wall as closely as possible. One hand was on my dagger under the folds of my belted dress. Underneath I wore pants in case I needed to fight.

The last time Lonnie had released the poor maligned sparrows to summon me, it was because he had royally screwed up a conjuring spell while trying to impress two visiting dukes. Lord Somerdon had just escaped the wizard lab as I came up the stairs. He foolishly decided on a drunken, overzealous welcome. By the time I convinced him to forgo his "welcome," the conjured baby dragons had set fire to the tapestries, Lonnie's clothing and Lord Grovert's very short beard. Lonnie hadn't known that even illusionary dragons, when spelled a certain way, came with very real flame.

Lonnie's door was open this time.

I sniffed. No noxious fumes. No pigeons or bats flying out for their lives.

I went in low and fast, like Father had taught me—taught both of us. Lonnie had lived with us until he started apprenticing at the castle. Sadly, the old wizard suffered an inexplicable magical accident within the year, and Lonnie was left with nothing but the magic he had learned from Mother. It should have been enough, but Lonnie used his free time to preen before the castle ladies rather than practice or try to grow his skills.

I pressed against the wall just inside the doorway, but even so, the sight before me almost caused my knees to buckle. My knife came out automatically, slicing through the unnecessary dress.

I wanted badly to close my eyes, but settled for closing my gaping mouth. My knees straightened of their own accord, deciding that bunched fighting muscles weren't called for.

"You blooming idiot," I hissed.

Lonnie and Kal, *the heir to the throne,* were encased in a magical ward that looked suspiciously cage-like. We had agreed long ago that while Mother and I would help with magic, it was far better for everyone that the king never discover our ability to assist. The arrangement provided a certain freedom. I continued to train with the dream of leaving Central and attending mage school in one of two schools that accepted females. Mother was able to live her life mostly unencumbered. Lonnie kept his job and should have had time to learn his craft.

So far, Lonnie had done nothing but waste his chance.

He stood inside a pulsing blue cage, his eyes bulging. After one frantic glance my way, he ignored me in favor of the outside wall.

I rolled without looking, putting myself closer to the cage than I would have liked. In this case, it was probably the safest spot because whoever had captured Lonnie and the prince wasn't likely to chance destroying the cage with a magic bolt.

The fire ball missed me by a feather. The smell of burned air wafted through the room. I was careful to avoid breathing the tainted ozone while I focused on the lady who had released the flaming blast. Her lithe form was topped by dark hair braided in a fancier style than my own. She jumped from the stone window. Her bluish-gray tunic and trousers blended well with the window ledge and had kept her hidden long enough to give her the opportunity to almost fry me when she threw flames.

Neither of us was dumb enough to underestimate the other. I circled away, holding my useless dagger. The sword she held announced her as the better fighter. The cage behind me...might or might not be her magic, but the fire had definitely come from her. The only thing that saved me from immediate death was that half her attention was on the doorway. She had no way of knowing that I was the only reinforcement coming.

"I don't know how they managed a call for help, but it will be their last," she said. Her booted foot slid gracefully towards me.

With the cage behind me, I had no choice but to dart sideways. "He isn't even good enough to call for help," I replied. As I turned slightly, I saw my cousin's still bulging eyes, but he wasn't talking. The ward was even better than I originally thought if it kept him from babbling excuses.

"But you came. That's unfortunate for you."

"Damn right it is." I sidled away from her weaving sword one more time, but there was little room left. She had me unless I was able to slip under her guard and out the door. Of course, I hadn't come completely unprepared. Danger was expected, especially that of a magical nature. I just hadn't expected the peril to be in the form of a complete stranger and someone who probably deserved to live.

"I don't suppose you'd just like to leave?" I offered.

My question surprised her. "And extract no revenge?"

"It's possible I can reverse whatever spell he used that has caused you...problems." Even though I didn't know the nature of Lonnie's transgression, I had reversed enough of his mistakes that I could probably fix this one in my sleep—if I lived long enough.

Her sword lowered the tiniest fraction. "Why was I called?"

"He called you here?" I dared a glance at the chalk scrawls on the floor that surrounded Lonnie and the prince. Sure enough, it looked like his work, careless about color, thin lines in some places, thicker in others. How had he then been trapped by his own spell? Idiot. I stifled a sigh. "If you put the sword away, I can probably figure out how to send you back."

Suspicious, she raised her weapon again.

"Look, I have no war with you." To show my good faith, I put my dagger away. In the process, I cut more of the dress because I wasn't used to wearing it these days. With my hand free, I palmed the crystal where I had stored enough energy to defend against an army of baby dragons, rats or men.

Luckily, her sword lowered. I backed to the cage. "It's going to take me a few minutes to read the spell. I have to figure out what he was doing before I can disassemble it."

"He called me from Wendal," she said.

"What?" I blinked in disbelief before turning to my cousin. "You called her from Wendal? Whatever for?" Something in the magic caused Lonnie's spelled-white hair to stand straight up. Kal's natural, dark-blond hair was tied back with a braided leather thong.

"I cannot imagine why they stole me here," she answered, since Lonnie couldn't. "The tall one reached into the cage and grabbed me. While he was half in, half out, I exchanged places with him." If being pulled into a strange room without warning wasn't enough of a clue, she had obviously recognized the diagram on the floor as an entrapment spell. When the prince broke through the circle, it probably wasn't hard for her to outmaneuver him and change places with him.

I smiled and almost laughed out loud, but the prince would throw me in the dungeon later if I let my mirth get the better of me. "How'd you get Lonnie in there?"

"Threw him."

Now I did laugh. "Is the silence spell yours?"

"No."

"So they didn't want you able to talk."

She shrugged and indicated her sword. "I don't need words." We watched each other, my heart no doubt beating louder than hers. She raised the sword slowly and slid it into a scabbard behind her back.

I gave her a nod as thanks.

With her sword away, I trusted her enough to move to one side of the circle and begin reading. On the far side, where I was fairly sure she couldn't throw anything at me without damaging the cage, I studied the spell. Of course, the innermost line was the calling, which meant that I risked destroying the cage and the speak spell when I sent her back. I didn't want to deal with all three spell-lines disintegrating at the same time if I could help it.

Since she hadn't attacked, I walked around, deciphering. If I hadn't trained with Lonnie, I never would have been able to read it so quickly. If I hadn't disabled the last conjuring he had done, I wouldn't have recognized Lonnie's idiot error either.

I dropped to my knees, my potential enemy taking on a whole new light. Something in my manner must have attracted her attention because she edged closer, doing her own studying. I glanced up at her and swallowed hard. "Seems they were looking for a beautiful maiden," I choked out, hoping she couldn't read the diagrams all that well.

"Perhaps that is why the tall one mistakenly called me his 'very own beauty' when he made a grab for me."

Even if she wasn't what I now suspected, calling her—or any

maiden—made no sense. "Where was he going to keep you? Locked in this diagram?"

We both stared at the two men trapped in the cage and then at each other. "He had sparrows locked up," she said. "I let them go."

So that was how Lonnie had gotten lucky enough to have the birds come to me for help. "Planning for the future has never been Lonnie's strong point." Neither was copying spells. He had obviously copied part of the one he had learned for calling baby dragons—only instead of altering all the parts to call a beautiful maiden, he had left in some very specific dragon lines.

I cleared my throat, very sure that this lady did not need my help getting home, by magic or mundane. "I can reverse the spell. You'll have to take it up with the prince's father—the king—if you want revenge." Most people thought those in Wendal had very interesting and sometimes powerful familiars, but in the deepest underground circles, those from Wendal were rumored to be changers; eagles, bears—and the most powerful, dragons. I knew without a doubt which rumor was true.

"I'm not getting back in that cage," the lady replied, her fingers twitching towards her sword.

"Don't worry, you don't have to be in the circle for me to reverse the spell." I could undo most of Lonnie's work without much study because he always used the same word of power to set a spell, another one to activate it and another one to disperse it. Total, he probably only used five words of power.

Lonnie had no doubt gotten in this mess by bragging that he could call a beautiful maiden any time he wanted. The prince had no doubt gotten in this mess because he was arrogant, believing he could ogle a fair maiden—or take advantage of her—and then send her back without a single consequence. He obviously didn't understand magic because he had stupidly stepped inside the diagram.

"Idiots," I muttered.

"Indeed. And how do I know that you are any better?"

My hands paused in the act of preparing to deactivate the spell. "That's a good question." I lowered my hands. "Do you want to just leave?"

Her eyes flicked towards the window. "Just like that?"

"I can get you out of the castle without any problems." I thought about my offer and corrected it. "I can get you out with a minimum of annoyances."

She almost smiled. "With a spell?"

I shook my head. "I was thinking on foot."

"That would be the safer. No offense."

In her boots, I don't think I'd let a total stranger attempt to reverse unknown magic either. I sighed. "Okay. Let's go."

She raised perfectly chiseled black eyebrows. "You're going to leave them there?"

I shrugged. "They're going to bellow and make stupid demands...hmm." I took in the spell lines again. "I'll release them in an hour once we are safely away." I hunted quickly through Lonnie's supplies, found what I wanted and laid a circle of white sand around the cage. I would never use sand outside where the wind could destroy it, but in this case, I needed a timed-link.

On the far side of the cage, I dribbled a tiny bit of sand against the speaking spell and then an almost-connecting line to the cage circle. I would tie all the new sand to an hourglass. When the sands ran down, the new sand would link, releasing the cage and the speaking spell.

As I set the sands, my hand froze over the diagrams, staring again at the dragon symbol. My heart beat harder as I realized a problem with letting her walk out. If she had to defend herself in a more public setting, it would be no small disaster. If she were somehow captured...either this time or the next...

It was a testament to Mother's training that my hand didn't shake as I reworked the two outer layers, quickly doing what needed to be done, hoping the woman from Wendal hadn't noticed my hesitation.

I sat back on my heels. "There is one problem." I stood and moved back towards her, ushering her to the far side of the room. Lowering my voice, I told her one of my concerns.

"He wouldn't try this again!"

"He's an idiot," I assured her. "If I don't destroy the diagram, he is likely to copy the thing. The prince has been humiliated, but at this point, the most he knows is where you are from and what you look like. But it wouldn't surprise me if he demanded my cousin try again, just to prove—"

"That they have no wish to live."

I nodded, sorry. "Leaving here with it still intact gives him too much time to memorize it or copy it. You could wait for me to destroy it, but the longer we delay, the greater the chance we'll be discovered. Once I start erasing the spell, I can't just send you back either. We could find ourselves severely limited."

Her eyes flashed. "I could go with my first plan, kill all of you and erase any signs of how I was called."

"You could." I still had my crystal with stored power. I might even have time to use it if necessary. Of course, she didn't deserve to die. Lonnie and the prince probably did, but I certainly didn't. There was really only one option. I didn't like to make choices for people or push my magic on them, but I didn't see any other way out. My stomach tightened. I kept my arms loose, never betraying my intent.

She withdrew her sword, slowly, deliberately.

With a flick of my wrist, I scattered the last bit of sand on her foot and uttered Lonnie's Word.

It was easy to hold my ground against the sudden, swift breeze because I expected it. The vacuum from her exit filled with air.

I stared at the empty space. My ears popped.

It would have been easier if she had trusted me. As it turned out, I was no different than Lonnie, forcing a spell on her, not allowing her the choice of how she returned to Wendal. The only good news was that my reversal would work a hell of a lot better than anything Lonnie ever tried.

I turned back to the two remaining spells that hadn't turned out quite as Lonnie had planned. "Idiot."

It was risky, reversing the calling by itself, but I needed her gone before they were released. Leaving them for any length of time, even stuck inside the ward, gave Lonnie too much time to make the situation worse.

My dress was a liability, so I dumped it in a corner before sweeping up the sand, working back to the circles. With excruciating care, I erased the inner spell, the calling. If my hand slipped, Lonnie or the prince could drag me into the cage—or if my body crossed the line, they could swap me in there as the lady from Wendal had done to them. I worked very, very precisely.

When every bit of the calling was cleared, I hunted through Lonnie's messy shelves until I found two partial bottles of wine that had turned to vinegar.

Some spells, especially after being activated, etched themselves lightly into stone. I wasn't taking any chances on this one being read back later. The vinegar soaked partially into the stone, destroying any lightly formed links.

After I was certain the inner spell was completely gone, I released the outer ring, the silencing spell.

The prince said two words: "Release me."

Lonnie babbled a cross between demands, excuses and threats.

I stood well back until Lonnie stopped talking.

"There will be no punishment for me. I'll have your word."

The prince snarled, "I promise you nothing, scullery. You'll release us *now*." He was his father's son, unreasonably angry at being rescued and by a girl no less. Too bad for him.

"I'd rather get the king. Maybe he will promise not to hurt me. I think I'll just tell him I found you when I came to visit my cousin."

Kal's mouth twitched and more dangerous than words, his brown eyes threatened retribution. The prince would have some explaining to do if the king found out he had been messing with wizard spells. He'd also be in trouble for letting himself be captured. Perhaps worst of all, even if the king believed I could help, he wouldn't accept my offer. That would mean the prince could be stuck a lot longer—like until the king hired another wizard.

"You won't be hurt," the prince finally ground out.

"No repercussions. No threats, no pleas to the king for rules that could affect me, no pranks, no thieves showing up to teach me a lesson, no dungeon. Your word on it."

He snarled, "My...word."

It sounded more like a question than a promise. I made a sign in the air, not even needing to pull from the crystal for such a light binding spell. "Say it. Give your word that no harm will come to me by your hands or by your means, no matter how casual."

To my eyes, the diagram glowed a light green. He stared at the space where I had drawn the magic, then at me. He started to speak, looking at Lonnie before facing me again. "You have my word. I will not harm you or attempt to harm you. By any means."

I whispered the word. The green glowed brighter and then curled itself into a ball. It raced towards the prince, disappearing just before the magic brushed along his neck. "Thank you."

I uttered Lonnie's word of power again. The bars of the cage snapped down, leaving dust upon the drawing.

The prince stalked past me without a word.

Lonnie sat in a heap without even exiting the diagram. He moaned.

I almost felt sorry for him, but not enough to change my mind. "I won't bring the sparrows back. Not now, not ever."

His head came up so fast it ought to have snapped. He gaped at me.

"No more, Lonnie." The male sparrow returned to me anytime Lonnie set the birds loose. I'd feed it and then it would go find Lonnie. It had been a game we discovered years ago. The last two times the bird had flown to me, it had stayed at the cottage even though I released it. I had finally brought it back to Lonnie, but it was obvious now that bird had been trying to tell me something. "Bittle won't be coming back."

"She killed him?"

"No," I said. "You did. You've killed any desire that bird had to be cared for by you. Even the bird realized that the only person you care about is you. Bittle has his flock to take care of. He isn't going to be your messenger anymore."

"But—"

"And I'm not going to come running to the rescue anymore either, Lonnie. You're the castle wizard. I'm not."

"You have to! I can't do this job on my own. I'll tell him that you have been helping me!"

"The king won't believe you if you tell him a woman has been helping you. And if you tell him that you can't do the job, he'll replace you. Either way, I'm off the hook. Lonnie, this was your chance. To do better than I could. Because," I swallowed my anger. "Because you're male and the king respected you automatically."

"I'll hire you," he said desperately. "I'm allowed an apprentice!"

On my worst day I could perform more spells than he could remember, total. "The prince is going to tell his father you are incompetent. You'd better be ready to prove otherwise."

Without another word, I left. Lonnie would sulk for days before he took action. It would be long enough for me to disappear. Bound word or not, I didn't trust the prince. Ready or not, it was time for mage school. If I could pass the entrance exam...there would be plenty of time to practice on the journey because it was a long one. I had just this day decided that I wanted to go to the school at the very corner of the Kingdom of Birk, far from Central, the main city where it seemed that I had spent enough of my life. Interestingly enough, the school was very close to Wendal.

Chapter 1 – Gorgon University One Year Later

The only good to come from leaving Central and going to mage school was being away from cousin Lonnie and castle politics. But I dearly missed my birds because message birds weren't allowed, not for mere students. My favorite sparrow had traveled with me until we were two days out from Gorgon University. Had it not been for Bittle, I might never have made it at all. He warned me about the wolves.

"Fly, fly!" He twittered nervously and hovered on the highest branch of a nearby pine.

Who was I to argue with a bird? It was darker than dusk, but not yet full night. I left the fire, pulled on my pack and climbed. I sat in the tree the entire night while the wolves prowled below. They knew I was there. One laughed at me, peeing on the trunk of the tree where I perched.

"Are you from Wendal?" I asked, innocently enough. When the wolf's golden yellow eyes glowed up at me, I knew I was pushing my luck, but grinned anyway. "I mean you no harm."

The wolf snorted.

Yeah. As if I were a threat to the wolf. But the wolf couldn't know for certain whether or not I was dangerous. It had to wonder how I had been clever enough to climb a tree before its arrival. Bittle didn't move around much at night, but he understood the warnings of the other animals and conveyed information to me if the tales were pertinent enough to him.

The wolf rolled its tongue, but then bared its teeth in a warning snarl.

"Yes, yes. I'm not stupid." My legs were firmly on the limb, not dangling. If the wolf was from Wendal, it could turn man. And if that were the case, it could climb the tree and do me harm, unlike the wolf form, which was mostly bound to the ground. I had little trouble understanding the wolf either way; like most animals, its feelings were fairly obvious to me. It would have been smarter to keep my ability secret, but even if the wolf was from Wendal, it would likely assume my conversation was luck, not real communication.

His eyes glowed a final warning as he sidled away from the tree. He didn't appear to be careless or stupid enough to take coincidence for granted. It would be a good thing if I didn't run into this wolf again.

* * *

Sitting in the school garden wedged between two thick lilac bushes, I almost wished the wolf had warned me to stay in Central and become a sensible seamstress. But even if he had been a shapeshifter, I doubt he concerned himself with the politics in the Kingdom of Birk or inept schools that seemed unable to impart wisdom on its students.

I crouched like a thief in hiding, waiting for dusk to settle deeper. It was too dark to continue reading the text I had filched from the library. A mage lamp would have solved the problem, but the whole point in concealing myself was to avoid getting caught trying to learn a new spell on my own. The light would be a dead giveaway.

Gorgon University was a newer school, founded just over a hundred and fifty years ago by Gorgon, a legendary mage from the Kingdom of Anton. The school had a reputation as forward thinking, but it was falling well short of its motto to teach not only well-known spells, but the coveted technique of creating brand new ones.

There were more rules than sense at the school. The two new spells I had learned happened only after I became desperate enough to "borrow" texts and read in secret. Any indication that a student could perform even the simplest of spells resulted in a lengthy interrogation.

I waited impatiently for darkness so that no one would witness me carrying the book back inside. The click of a key turning in a lock, followed by the squeak of rusty hinges on a rarely used door near the bushes interrupted my stupor.

I huddled down even lower inside my carved out hiding spot.

A man with a long dark cloak shuffled out of the door backwards. He complicated his situation by dropping his half of a long bundle. The bulky package immediately began struggling against the ropes and a thick blanket that wrapped it from head to neck. A loose hood covered the prisoner's head.

My eyes widened, but with all the leaves in front of my face, it wasn't possible to see very well. My heart tripped over itself. Very carefully, I moved a single branch.

Muffled protests came from the trussed-up captive. A shorter man than the first pushed the prisoner's legs free of the door. He was roundly kicked for his mistake of assuming the captive would not fight.

I kept my breathing completely quiet, smelling the damp earth and decaying leaves that were now very close to my face. *Who was it?*

The biggest guy grabbed the shoulders of the trapped person and lifted again, but with a violent twist, the captive yanked free. The hood caught on the man's sword sheath and pulled loose.

Despite the heavy gag, I recognized Irwin. His face was closer to me than it would have been had I been standing instead of flattened behind the bushes. His eyes bulged as he fought for his life. One ear was dark with blood.

I let the branch go and reached for the hidden yellow crystal sewn into my tunic. It was well concealed because if anyone at the school caught me with it, the questions would go on forever. First year students weren't allowed any elements that could store power or spells. We supposedly weren't trained enough.

In the dimming light, Irwin may have seen my face or maybe he spotted the lilac branch as it moved. His eyes were already bulging and the sounds he made through the gag would have been the same whether he saw me or not.

I had only spoken to Irwin once, just a week ago. He had caught me returning a filched text to the library. The ponderous wooden door should have been closed and locked—it was almost always locked, even before curfew. With me half slipping out of it, the door obviously wasn't secured.

Irwin had whispered, "Back inside, quick!"

I had obeyed, expecting him to duck inside with me, but he had grabbed the door from my unresisting hand and pulled it closed.

There was nothing but silence for a while and then his voice came through the thick oak door. "Too much sword practice and my legs cramp up. Trying to walk it off. "

A strident male voice berated him about curfew, responsibility and studying spells harder so he wouldn't be reliant on his sword.

Irwin murmured apologies and for his trouble, he received assurances he would be getting demerits on his record.

He was lucky he was a noble paying exorbitant tuition. If they had caught me or the two of us together, I knew who would have gotten the worst end of it. If they had seen me coming out of the library, they'd have packed my bags for me.

I planned to wait for a long time to make sure the danger was past, but to my surprise, within a minute or two, a light tap brushed the door. It opened and Irwin slipped inside.

He grinned. "May I escort you upstairs? We'll need to hurry. The mage-master has been meeting with half the staff tonight. The hallways are busy."

"What's going on?"

He shrugged. "No idea. Some strangers arrived late. I caught wind of happenings when I noticed strange mounts in the stables. I was headed back to my rooms when I ran into you." He cracked the door a mere slit and checked the hallway.

We scooted out, and he waited for me to lock the library.

We practically flew through the hallways and up the stairs. Nobles often had privileges the rest of us didn't, but if he were caught a second time and with me in tow, I hoped he had a better excuse ready than cramping muscles.

At my dorm room, he gave me an undeserved half bow and a smile before trotting off to the stairwell that led up to the next level where he had private rooms.

Perhaps he never mentioned my secret because he had been coming in a back exit that was used to access the stables, a place where he had no legitimate business at that hour. The nobles had someone to care for their mounts and the rest of us were allocated time in very firmly kept schedules.

He wasn't keeping a schedule now, that was for sure. The two men picked him back up and hurried along the wall until they reached the outer gate.

I edged free of the bushes, expecting a few precious seconds to sneak up on them, but the gate didn't slow them down at all. It was unlocked. They were through it and behind the stone wall before I went more than two steps.

The few defense spells I knew required preparation. They wouldn't work from a distance. Flames were useless unless one of them stood still while I set him afire. Light and illusion...if only there had been time to set a spell ahead of time, I could have blasted them across the garden.

As I glided forward as fast as possible, their voices carried over the wall. "Ain't no one gonna want to marry a Wendal girl. No way I'd take a man over there."

"We only...as far as..." the other responded, his voice fading in and out as they moved off.

My attention was already riveted, but I froze and held my breath trying to hear better. Part of the reason I had chosen Gorgon Uni was because cousin Lonnie had called a woman from Wendal for the prince.

Even before that incident, rumors of witches, familiars and shifters had me fascinated by the region. Now thieves were dragging Irwin off to Wendal?

But why? It was becoming increasingly clear that someone or several someones wanted an alignment with Wendal. Or maybe a war. "Oh, Irwin, you are in trouble, indeed."

I kept low and scurried to the gate. There were two of them and one of me...and they had been given a key to one of the outside doors. Who here had given it to them?

At the gate I paused to listen, but only the wind spoke now. A quick peek through the metal frame revealed the empty pasture and the forest beyond.

It was now too dark to see footprints. Had they horses waiting? It would make sense. Who had let them in and told them where to find Irwin?

If there had been a chance to help, I had blown it. They must have had horses even though I hadn't heard them.

Instead of returning to the library, I rushed upstairs to my room, book and all. Throwing open the wooden shutters, I despaired. It was too dark to make out cloaked thieves rushing off with their prize. No telling which direction they had taken. It was too late to find a bird to follow.

I paced. The scant rug had been worn bare long before my arrival, but my fretting was going to leave it even more threadbare.

"Who kidnapped Irwin, and what does Wendal have to do with anything?" There was no one to answer me. Thankfully, my roommate was off in a study group even though the approved texts were missing half their pages. "I could follow. Let those who care about him know where he has been taken. It wouldn't be more than a missed day of study..." If I didn't make it back before morning, I'd be kicked out of school.

"After I find out what has happened to Irwin, I can apply to a new school. Go somewhere better that actually teaches." But getting into Gorgon had been difficult enough. My parents had enough merchant skills to do well enough in Central, but without the haphazard education I had gained from helping Lonnie, plus a scholarship because he was the castle wizard, I wouldn't be here. We couldn't afford the expensive lessons that most students received before applying to the universities.

At eighteen summers, I was a year or three younger than many of the mages-in-training and had far less formal education. Passing the university level exams had tested me sorely. "I don't even know Irwin, anyway." But what if it had been me carted off into the night by dangerous men? Not likely. I wasn't important enough to kidnap. "They'll likely kill him. Of course, I cannot stop them anyway."

But in the end, I knew I would go. "I'll see where they have taken him and be back before morning." The hard part would be finding his trail.

"I'm going to need supplies." Difficult, that. Grimly determined, I pulled my pack from under the bed. Donning my old clothes was a vast improvement over the scratchy wool uniform. It wasn't just that mother could out-sew most merchants either; it was the lack of quality of the uniform cloth.

Nothing here made sense. Instead of learning, we were shuffled from class to class like chickens to new pens. If anything, the teachers seemed bent on bleeding out any talent. While those without magical ability or interest were quite common all over Birk, it was a mystery how at least four student teachers became such without knowing a single spell.

Maybe I just didn't belong here. My training had rather large gaps, and I tended to fail some of the simple tests even though I could work far more complicated spells.

It was foolish to worry about it now given what I was about to do.

I opened the door to the hallway and nearly ran into the mage-master's wife, Teal, as she rushed through the corridor. She emitted a half-swallowed scream and almost dropped a partially covered crystal mage light. She was too startled to notice my lack of uniform. I allowed my pack to slide off my shoulder and land behind the door where she couldn't see it.

"Mage-Master Alcen missed supper again," Teal said breathlessly. As she turned back to the open hallway, one calloused hand pushed a curl of shocking white hair away from a face too young for it. "Need sausage and cheese."

If she was on her way to the kitchens, there went my plans to filch even a small cache of traveling supplies. I could hardly stuff my bag full in front of the head mistress. Sadly, of all the places in the school, the kitchen was guarded the most heavily. Heaven forfend someone get access to a metal spoon that might be used to store energy for a spell.

I watched her hurry off.

"Bother." I picked up my pack and noted my last three arrows sticking out of their special sleeve. The bow was attached to the side of the pack and even if it did fit inside, putting it there was a waste of time.

I wrapped my pack and bow in my cloak and slung it over my shoulder like a laundry bag. It was too late to be doing laundry. The best I could hope for was that no one would recognize me half hidden behind the pack.

I got moving.

The stables weren't heavily guarded; most of the students took little interest in their mounts and even so, where would they go?

Somewhere, apparently. Brittany, my roommate, had beaten me down there. Her long black hair was shoved under a hat. The pants and tunic she had stolen fit too loosely on her wiry frame. She had her mount already saddled.

"Late to be traveling, isn't it?" She spun around low and ready for a fight, which was a little surprising since most students came from upper-class families who were able to hire protection if necessary. Unlike me, she was at least related to someone of importance, although she was far enough down the line that she didn't rate her own rooms. The way she held her knife told me she knew how to use it and well.

I slipped quickly out of reach.

She snarled, "If you've been paid to delay me from rescuing Irwin, take the money and run. You'll not win."

I backed away and opened a stall door between us for protection. She had just admitted why she was down here and with no prompting from me. One confession deserved another. "I'm not working for anyone. I thought I'd find out enough to send a bird messenger to someone who cared."

She checked the outside entrance before flicking her eyes back at me. "How do you know someone took him if you weren't sent to stop me?"

"I was in the garden studying. They walked right past me with Irwin tied down tighter than a hog on roast day."

"Bastards! If they want a scapegoat to control, they can pick one of the others. Stay out of my way. I'm going after him."

I pondered that. Irwin was one of the school's most valuable assets, potentially in line for his own piece of the kingdom if all went well, but that did not tell me how she was involved. "I thought you were the daughter of Duke...Wellingham?" I guessed badly.

Her eyes narrowed. "Try again."

"Well, you aren't from Central and neither is Irwin." Come to think of it, I couldn't name the exact territory from which Irwin hailed. Hmm. I didn't put much stock in the status of the nobles because I wasn't one and stood to gain nothing from their jockeying for position, but it was odd that in all the mutterings, I couldn't place either of them more closely than "north." Had Brittany ever told me where she was from? Or had she purposely evaded the question by acting as if I should know?

"Just stay out of my way. Go back inside and don't tell anyone I've gone. You'll be perfectly safe." She stopped talking on a gasp. In a strained voice, she continued, "Could worse luck possibly fall?"

I turned and saw the cause of Brittany's alarm. "Hewitt!" The son of Mage-Master Alcen gazed at us from the stable door. He chewed on his fist. At four years of age, he shouldn't have been awake and certainly not wandering about unattended.

"Hewitt, what are you doing here?" I whispered.

He bent stubby knees to trail his finger along the dirt floor. His drawing was too deliberate to be a child playing.

"You know where Irwin has been taken," I guessed, quickly making my way to him. "Hewitt, tell me and save us all the trouble."

He shook his head. "Must go," he said before turning his fist back into a nervous meal.

I stared into his intelligent eyes and despaired. Few others acknowledged he was a seer; his father and mother both denied the signs. Twice I'd seen him work his tricks. The first time was in the garden. Hewitt came running out of the school and searched quickly until he found a long thin stick. He placed his find just so, partially in the shade of an apple tree. Then he ran back inside.

I had continued studying my borrowed library text, quite hidden from view. A half hour later, Hewitt reappeared behind his father, Master Alcen. The mage-master was cleaner than a homeless beggar but just as disheveled. His beady hawk eyes missed very little, but his long white hair was so long and tangled, it hid the parts of his face that his flowing beard and mustache did not. Loose robes threatened to drop off behind him as he wandered the garden, studying his options.

Master Alcen finally picked Hewitt up and settled him under the apple tree. "You stay here and enjoy the sunshine. Da has things to do." The mage-master then drew a large containment spell around the tree and Hewitt. He left the boy with toys and a snack.

Once Master Alcen had safely disappeared, Hewitt ate his snack and then crouched near the stick. It lay underneath the glyphs the mage-master had drawn. Hewitt carefully turned the stick, much like he was opening a door—or in this case the circle. With gleeful delight, he stepped out of his confinement.

Though I had made not a single sound, Hewitt knew I was in the garden. He disappeared inside the school for a bit, stole a snack from somewhere and then crawled between the lilacs to share his largess with me.

This dark night, he was more demanding. He raised his hands and let them flop back to his sides. "Mama won't take me. You will."

"We'll be flogged to within an inch of our lives," Brittany said in horror. "And you two will only slow me down and cause the alarm to be sounded."

Hewitt tugged my arm. "Mama comes. Fire starts."

I had no idea what he was talking about. "What fire?"

"Mama leaves. Hurry!"

"Drat!" Hewitt's mother was already up and about; I'd just seen her. Perhaps she had really been searching for her wayward son, but didn't want to admit he was missing. I rushed to the end of the stalls to my pony. "Do you have an extra mount for Irwin?"

"I don't have time for this," Brittany warned.

"You won't know where to find Irwin unless we follow Hewitt," I pointed out. "Hewitt wouldn't be here if we didn't need him. It's the way of seers."

Brittany ground her teeth. "I have another mount for Irwin."

Getting through the outer gates was not as hard as it should have been, but since someone had kidnapped Irwin, the complete lack of security was one more suspicious sign that someone at the school was complicit.

Once outside the gates, I secured Hewitt on the horse with Brittany's supplies. Luckily she had found a way to procure food. Hewitt was nothing more than another small lump of supplies except for the brightness of his face peering out from dark curls. "Keep your head on the pack," I instructed.

He smiled and obediently pillowed his head.

"I may kill Irwin myself for this mess," Brittany muttered.

Once safely into the trees, Brittany asked, "Hewitt would tell us if we were going the wrong way?"

"Who can know?" But I knew. The kid had more than vague dreams. He had visions even in the light of day that kept him out of trouble. I looked back in the direction of the university. No fire. What fire had he been talking about? Perhaps he meant the bonfire they'd start when they decided to burn me for my stupidity.

Traveling in the dark was just one more foolish decision, but luckily my mount was more hardy pony than high-bred. She was sure-footed and calm. Brittany's mounts were taller and less stout, but they too plodded along in no particular hurry or worry.

Hewitt whimpered in his sleep anytime we strayed from a westerly path.

"How did you know someone had kidnapped Irwin?" I asked.

My only answer was the clop of hooves against the ground. Brittany casually leaned forward as if to miss a low-hanging branch, but I saw her reach into her boot. Perhaps I shouldn't have asked. My pony was plodding half behind hers, but if her boot housed a throwing dagger, my current position wouldn't save me.

Her head never twisted my way, and luckily her arms stayed forward. My heart beat so loudly, I nearly missed her answer. "I'm his sister. I check on him often."

It would be rude of me to point out that her story couldn't possibly be true. If she was his sister, she'd have private rooms like he did. It would have been more believable if she had claimed a romantic tryst with him.

Hewitt mumbled something sleepily, but it was little more than half a giggle.

"How many men were there?" Brittany finally asked.

I had nothing to hide and no reason to keep the information from her. She'd known me for the entire year. I'd given her no reason to mistrust me and wasn't about to now, not with her ready to skewer me. "Two. A large guy, easily a foot or more taller than myself and a short stocky one who complained about the task."

"Was it Camden?"

"Camden?" I repeated. "Who is he? A teacher?" Someone inside the school had to have been helping, but neither man had acted like a student or a teacher. I knew most of the help, including the boys in the stable and it hadn't been any of them.

Brittany kept her attention on picking out a path through the heavy woods. "Camden was a student a long while back, but he...visited now and then. Very tall, brown hair, almost always tied back with a heavy gold clip. He complains a great deal, carries a sword and swaggers constantly."

Now how would she know a former student and so well that she could describe him in such detail? Camden, if it had been he, had not used magic and had left the distinct impression of thug rather than student, but then, he'd been in the middle of kidnapping Irwin, not reading a textbook. "They both wore heavy cloaks. The tall one did have a sword but with Irwin between them, no one was swaggering. It was near dark out. Could be him, although it was the shorter one doing the complaining about taking someone to Wendal."

When she was silent for some time, I finally asked, "Why would anyone want to drag him off to Wendal?"

"Stupidity. Sheer stupidity."

It was, apparently, the only answer she was going to give. The occasional snap of a twig under horse hooves filled in the quiet around us. To my relief, Brittany did lean back to her boot. Apparently my answers had been good enough to ward off an immediate fight.

She rode well and the mounts she had brought along were very good stock. Irwin was a noble. The sister lie reeked of hiding something, but she also wasn't a bawling lover stealing away to rescue him. The only part I believed was that she checked on him often.

By the time the moon reached its peak, I faced facts. I had left the school, and my chances of sneaking back unnoticed became more and more unlikely with each step, no matter what I had told myself earlier. Without proper training as a mage, I could aspire to no more than living in the country and hoping a low noble became my patron in exchange for a spell or three that he couldn't otherwise afford. Moving back to Central was laughable. Lonnie would plague me with threats in order to gain my help—assistance and spells he never paid for. I had put that game behind me with great relief, and I wasn't crawling back now.

Maybe, somehow, another mage school would accept me.

I stifled a worried groan. Training as a seamstress like my mother would have been far better than this disaster. Too many untrained mages ended up barely able to recharge crystal lanterns and living in a dungeon while they attempted the bidding of some crazy politician. Want to eat? Do the spell. Can't? You'll stay here and rot.

Nobles always appeared to have it much better, but Irwin had been trussed up like any peasant and hustled out of the school under cover of darkness. If I hadn't been sitting in the garden contemplating my stolen library text, I'd be in bed now, blissfully unaware. Unless Hewitt had come and dragged me out anyway.

The four-year-old must have known I was thinking about him because his sleepy eyes blinked at me when I turned to check on him. He sat up, but otherwise stayed perfectly still. He listened to sounds or sights only a seer could sense before flopping his head back down without a word.

His actions did nothing to dispel my visions of a lonely dungeon in my future.

We plodded onward, taking no breaks and having no real evidence we were headed the right way, but by the time the light of dawn threatened the skyline, there was no denying we were headed for the village of Glaston. It directly bordered Wendal unless you counted the no-man's zone that ran a mile the entire width of the border.

As we approached the thinning trees closer to the village, sounds carried in the morning air, including church bells. The scene, when we finally topped the hill, took my breath away. "Oh no!" I had thought whoever took Irwin would hide him away until a marriage could be arranged, but from the activity, it was obvious a large celebration was about to take place.

"This was well-planned ahead of time," Brittany muttered, surveying the throngs of people below. The entire village was dressed in finery and milling about. Industrious merchants were selling wares to the early morning crowds. Many of the villagers were meandering happily towards the church that rose out of a rocky outcropping to the north of the village.

"Why would anyone go to so much trouble?"

"Witnesses. Enough hoopla to make sure no one could deny it happened. People make money on an event, they talk about it. They owe favors to those who brought the business."

"I'm not so sure rescuing him is possible." In fact, I was damned certain it was impossible. "Not worth our lives." When that elicited no response, I added, "Why does everyone want to marry someone from Wendal so badly?"

She shot me a look, probably meant to be condescending. "You seem to know rather more than you should for one who exists only on scholarship."

"No, I'm not highborn." I didn't view that as a detriment most of the time and certainly not at this moment. Who wanted to be kidnapped, forced into marriage and politics? It hadn't worked out all that well for cousin Lonnie. My family had always been happy on the fringes. We paid our taxes and were talented enough to benefit without bothering to be drawn into the political arena.

"What is that group of horses? Is it Irwin?" Brittany strained tall in her saddle, but it wasn't enough. "Wait here! I'm going to climb!" She wrapped one gloved hand around a low hanging maple branch and hopped from the lower branches to the middle quickly. She climbed well for a noble. "It's horses all right and," she choked on a deep breath, "there's a white one, draped in purple and red!"

"A bishop?" Most priests were lucky to ride a donkey. Only a bishop would ride such a finely bred mount. "They bothered to get a bishop to witness a coerced marriage?" Someone wanted this marriage recorded very badly.

"The procession is moving," Brittany said. "If we hurry, we can make it to the church ahead of them. She dropped from her perch, back onto her mount.

"Then what? Steal him at knife point?" How could she possibly hope to stop the thing?

The church had been built as a last stand, atop a cliff. I followed Brittany across the opposite ridge and then down the far side. From there we could climb to the church. "There's always the bell tower," I mused. "I can get inside and hide there before the ceremony starts. But then what?" I glanced back at Hewitt, who was sitting astride eagerly now. "You've brought us here. If you've any final advice, now would be a great time to hear it."

Hewitt smiled placidly.

He was nothing but trouble. We hadn't taken him far from his parents, and the lie of claiming to have found him would be easy enough. But there was still the matter of *returning* him. How to get Hewitt back to the school? How to get me into another school? I believed in following magic, but he had already pushed things way past reasonable.

Brittany dismounted and rummaged in her pack. She extracted a long sling and a shorter one. Both disappeared under her tunic. She left Hewitt's little hands full of food.

I stashed my bow and arrows under my tunic as well, noting that Brittany's loose-fitting clothes worked better for the task than my better fitting ones. Perhaps hers weren't stolen wares after all.

Brittany said, "You'll need to create your own distractions and protect yourself."

"Can you use that sling to shoot kindling into the church? The wooden shutters on the side will be open to let in light and air. Your sling should be accurate enough to get something through."

She stared down at her weapon. "The leather on the sling might smother any fire."

"The church will have a glass window or two near the altar. I can't break them with arrows. Your sling and a well-shot stone could handle that."

"There's more lead in those windows than in a good pot! The stones are likely to come right back on my head."

"Do your best," I suggested. I didn't have any better ideas and as plans went, ours were about as useful as milk left in the sun all day.

Chapter 2

Time was not on our side. Even as we reached the pinnacle where the church sat like a craggy hand on the end of a very fat arm, the crowds approached the bottom of the mountainside.

"To whatever end." Brittany clutched my shoulder tightly for a scant second.

"I'll install myself in the tower before the ceremony begins." I had no idea what I'd do once there, but if Brittany created enough of a disturbance and Irwin wasn't bound hand and foot for his own wedding, he might be able to make good on an escape.

I left Brittany muttering. If she were smart, she'd go straight back to the horses and ride away like the wind.

The bell ringer continued to announce the impending nuptials. A few hired mercenaries lined the rough cobblestones at the west entrance. Expecting villagers, they paid me scant attention.

I was nothing more than a young boy on an important mission. Without pausing, I scurried up the two steps into the simple nave. A small vestibule exited from either side of the sanctuary area at the front of the church. On the right, the bell tower formed a square wing.

As my eyes adjusted to the dim light, I spotted the ladder at the back of the church. The stone bell tower had no stairs, but the ladder was more than serviceable as a way through the hole to the back loft.

I climbed.

The first floor room had one window to the outside and a much wider one overlooking the nave. The priest could lecture from here, but it was really for calling instructions to those huddled in the church during a siege. Another ladder led to an upper chamber where the bell-boy rang the bells hard.

I checked the outside window. There was no way to fend off the entire village, especially with only three lowly arrows. They were spelled for accuracy, but shooting three into this crowd wouldn't even buy Irwin time.

No, only a more secure target, one that was close, like Irwin himself, would halt the wedding.

I took myself across the dirty floor to the opening that overlooked the nave. The crowds arrived, happy to gather and gossip.

I kept to the side, easily able to see the large altar. The bishop stepped from one of the small side rooms, his elegant robes marking him as impressive and important. My heart missed a beat when Irwin was pushed out behind him. The ropes at his wrists were tucked mostly under his school uniform, but for anyone paying attention it was obvious he was tied. Then again, he only needed his legs to run. His eyes scanned the crowds and paused at the mercenaries guarding the back entrance.

"You'll have to be swift," I muttered, knowing that even if Brittany caused a distraction, escape wasn't likely, not unless I shot the bishop and stopped the wedding cold. Leaving school was one thing. Taking Hewitt was more unforgivable, even if that was never tied to us. But shooting a bishop? I may as well jump from the window now and save myself a hanging.

My stomach clenched as the church filled. The bishop began his blessings. The bride, tall and proud, was deposited next to Irwin by a large warrior dressed in green and gold. Not only were the bride's hands bound, but ropes kept her arms pinned to her sides. The ties wound all the way down her legs. A dark green cloak draped around her shoulders hid the restraints as soon as the warrior pivoted her to face the altar. The sight of her face as she was turned away set my heart pounding.

"Not you again!" I whispered, disbelieving. It was the same woman, the one cousin Lonnie had called from Wendal. Her black locks were only partially braided and her face was badly scraped on one side. Half a dark eyebrow had been singed off, but she still stood proud, her blackened eyes threatening all the men who were out of her reach.

She was also out of time. The choice was too difficult. "Do I shoot Irwin?" That would solve the problem. She couldn't marry a dead man. If I shot at anyone else, what good would it do? I'd hang for killing the bishop. There were too many warriors to attack and once they killed me, the wedding would go on. Taking a chance on killing the bride seemed grossly unfair.

Well then, Irwin, you should have been born a peasant. I couldn't swear that the bride was innocent, but I still owed her for Lonnie's stupidity. If not that, I had tricked her when I sent her back to Wendal. Of course, Irwin didn't deserve to die either.

Steady. Spelled arrows or not, I could ill afford to miss.

The first arrow did go left of its mark because Irwin leaned over in a coughing fit just as I fired. The arrow would go where it was aimed, but that didn't mean the spell would dive down after its target. Luckily, I had trained relentlessly. Once committed, it was but a fluid motion to ready the next.

Irwin spied the first arrow as it landed in the altar with a thunk. He swiveled in surprise. The bishop, whose robe had been sliced by the arrow, cowered on the floor, a reasonable place given that the arrow had narrowly missed something more vital.

"Hold still, Irwin. I will save you yet."

The next arrow struck true as Irwin made himself an easier target, flinging his bound arms in front of his bride.

Excellent. My arrow landed solidly in his shoulder. He screamed and fell backwards.

I allowed one shuddering breath, but the thought of missing and killing him outright made spots dance in front of my eyes.

Thankfully, Brittany delivered the promised distraction. Smoke arrived on the backs of two flaming bundles of straw. They landed square in the center of the crowd. Even better, the glass window in the front shattered, a crashing cascade.

When the window broke, the bishop gave a shriek of agony. Glass was expensive and replacing it would mean less money in his coffers.

More missiles came through the broken window, providing me the opportunity to join the crowd as though fleeing. Just as I grabbed the ladder, the small head of the bell ringer peered upside-down from the upper bell chamber. Startled, I missed the ladder step and slid painfully to the bottom floor. The unforgiving stone jarred my bones all the way to my teeth.

I could hear Irwin yelling as though the arrow had pierced his heart. Women, protected by the men, rushed outside, away from the smoke. Soon enough it would occur to someone that although a few smoking sticks had come from outside, the missile that had hit Irwin had come from the tower.

The bishop peeked from behind the altar, shouting orders at the warrior crouched next to the bride. The burly man's green and gold tunic was decorated with enough fancy embroidery that it was obvious he was not a lowly, hired soldier.

Green and gold? I inspected Irwin again, but he still wore the school uniform. "North," I muttered and then my eyes widened, returning to the warrior. There were two kingdoms to the north of Birk and one of them flew a flag of green and gold. "You aren't from the kingdom of Birk at all!" His colors indicated he was from Anton. His brown hair was pulled back and, as Brittany had mentioned, tightly secured with a gold clasp. He wielded a sword that contained at least one large jewel in the pommel. Despite the possible threat of arrows, he didn't falter. His blade held steady on the snarling bride-to-be.

As I gained my feet, his roving eyes spotted me. The green orbs narrowed suspiciously when he noticed the ladder behind me. He turned his attention to the window opening where I had recently stood. He glanced back and forth once. The connection was made.

I turned to run. In one motion, the Anton warrior flung aside a lingering bystander and marched straight at me. It was far too late to join the crowds now. He would kill me long before he bothered to find out I was a nobody who didn't even know what was going on.

Well, all's hell that ends there. The crowds blocked the door anyway. I spun back around and notched my third arrow.

With a roar, he charged, his sword arm taking my last, hopeless missile. It barely damaged the large man, slicing through his upper arm but not slowing him much. His blade swept back fast, and unlike any wooden practice sword, flashed towards my neck.

I dove for his legs, hoping to roll under or between them. My hand went into a pocket and grasped one of my crystals. It stored energy, and this close to him a word of power from me would blast him backwards. I might then have time to run.

My body rolled into his solid leather boot, hitting sooner and harder than I expected. "Ooof!" All the air in my lungs whooshed out. His legs didn't budge, and I was left gasping.

He stopped me from getting up when he toppled forward like a felled tree.

At first, through a haze of gulping air, I assumed I had somehow unbalanced him, but then Brittany appeared. She smiled an evil grimace and lowered her sling, stashing it under her tunic. Ducking her head, she hissed, "Camden. Nothing but a miserable, failed wizard."

Her eyes searched and found Irwin. She had seen my bow and arrows, smaller than any warrior would carry. With a snarl, she accused me. "You shot him??? How could you do something so dimwitted?"

I untangled myself from the man's boots and jumped up. I nearly fell back down again when Hewitt poked his head from behind Brittany.

Calm as ever, he toddled up to the felled Anton swordsman, dragging our attention with him. Hewitt's hand hovered, moving back and forth across the man's chest, undecided where to land.

"Should we kill him?" Brittany asked. "He deserves it, I admit. He is nothing but a thief, living off a single spell he stole eons ago. He makes a better warrior than mage, and if his thievery at last requires his death, so be it."

Hewitt shook his head. He gathered the man's green tunic in his little fist and twisted it about.

"Ah. Treasure is it?" I guessed. A quick inspection found the lump without much trouble. A single slice from my dagger freed it.

The ring puzzled me. The blue stone was in a setting carved into the likeness of a lion with wings. "This is not Glaston's symbol. Nor does it belong to Anton or Birk."

"Of course not," an imperious voice interrupted.

I stiffened, ready to use the dagger, but the bishop was unarmed.

"I'll take that." He held out his hand towards the ring.

"Never!" I backed away. "I don't know why you want it, but I am pretty sure you don't deserve it."

Hewitt shook his head. "Not now," I snapped. "You are insane if you think I will give it to this man!"

Hewitt reached up and snatched the ring even as I moved to put it on one of my own fingers. Quick as a rabbit, he scurried up the nave. The bishop made a grab for him, but Brittany stuck out her foot and tangled it in his robes.

We both flanked the boy swiftly, catching up with him halfway to the altar.

Irwin had stopped shouting and rested against the short stair. "I'm too injured to marry," he declared.

When the dark-haired bride saw what Hewitt offered, she seized the ring with cramped fingers. Even that movement nearly tipped her over.

"Not bound for long," she said.

Irwin groaned loudly, but was ignored.

The moment the bride-to-be slid the ring across her slim finger, the blue stone flared. "I'll not have him," she told the bishop. "Not now, not ever. Do not try your tricks again."

"Don't be a fool, girl!"

The ring sparked. "Who is the fool?" she snarled. She raised her arms as if the ropes were not there. In her place, a dragon just smaller than my stout pony rose. Her talons narrowly missed the bishop as she gained height.

"Why did she need the ring?" The women of Wendal weren't tied to objects, not that I had ever heard. Yet the bishop wanted the ring. Hmm. "You helped kidnap a maiden from Wendal to marry Irwin? Why? He's not that highly ranked."

I caught Brittany's eyes, but she quickly lowered them. The colors of the warrior were Anton. And Brittany had been keeping an eye on Irwin. She was far too competent to be merely a romantic companion or a sister. "I suppose Irwin *is* highly ranked." He had to be one of the princes of Anton. Why he was at mage school was not entirely clear. It was possible the king of Anton wanted one of his sons trained as a mage. But it was also possible Irwin was hiding out either to stall an unwanted marriage, be protected from a death threat—or wait for the right marriage offer to appear. Someone had found him and decided on a marriage offer, that was for sure.

"I merely agreed to perform a nice wedding ceremony!" the bishop shrieked.

I snorted. "The warrior bound her to that ring somehow. It forced her to do his bidding, didn't it?"

"She wanted to marry him!"

"Yeah, that would be why she had to be tied for her own wedding."

The dragon had her own opinion. From her precarious perch on the wing of a carved angel that was too small to support her full bulk, she emitted a scream of outrage.

I still wanted answers. "You were going force her into marriage. And then what?"

The bishop's lip curled. "You interfere where you don't belong. You—"

The dragon dove, her talons raking across the bishop's face. The purple-scaled beast went for his eyes, wings battling furiously, claws tearing.

The man never got more than two steps towards the door before the dragon snapped his neck.

With a flick of its tail, the dragon quickly changed directions, diving towards Irwin.

"Oh," Brittany pleaded, "don't hurt him after all I've been through to save him! He was not in on the plan. He did not want to marry you. No offense. An alignment can be made with Wendal, but not through a forced marriage! I swear Camden didn't have the ability to perform the magic that trapped you either, even if he did drag Irwin here." Brittany stopped begging when the dragon landed peacefully near Irwin.

A huge eyeball studied him first, then switched to me. Peevishly, it pecked at Irwin's tunic, the blue and gold of the school uniform dribbled with blood from his injured arm.

The dragon looked at me again, a question in her eyes. I finally understood. "No, I wasn't trying to kill him. I was hoping if he were injured it would be enough of a distraction that you or he could run. I didn't know you were bound to a ring."

With a chirp, the former bride-to-be inclined her iridescent head. Without wasting any additional time, she took to the air. The beat of her wings nearly flattened us before she disappeared through the broken glass window.

Brittany sighed with relief. "We are lucky she left Irwin alive."

"Her quarrel was not with him," I said.

Hewitt knelt next to Irwin and patted his shoulder.

I collected the arrow that wasn't stuck in anyone and said, "I wish someone would tell me what is going on."

"Really," Brittany drew herself back into her royal attitude. "Now isn't the time."

Given that we were standing in a church with a dead bishop, an injured royal and a dead or badly injured Anton warrior, she had a point.

And getting out was never as easy as getting in.

Chapter 3

There was no cover of darkness to help us. The villagers hadn't gone far after escaping the church either. Several had seen the dragon fly off. From the mutterings, they were far more offended by it than the disruption of the wedding, and they hadn't even seen the dead bishop yet, a very obvious casualty of the creature.

Hewitt was no help at all. He found my hand with his and waited for me to make a decision.

"Come on, then." Maybe hiding behind Hewitt was the right answer. Just another mother...in pants at a wedding. I reached to my head, forgetting for a moment that I had left my cloak with the horses. "Oh, bother."

From behind me, Irwin let out a horrific scream that cut off rather too suddenly. I turned back to find a pale and sweating Brittany holding my broken arrow. "It had to come out."

"You could have untied his hands first."

I stepped back over and slashed at his bound hands with my dagger. Maybe by the time he regained consciousness, his fingers would have circulation again. I checked the wound. It wasn't great.

"You shouldn't have shot him!" Brittany collapsed next to him, hysteria about two steps behind her. "Now what are we going to do? We've got to find a healer."

"Can you get him back to the school?"

Her brown eyes rolled wildly. "It's not safe for him! Camden found him there!"

"The dragon is freed. They have no reason to kidnap him again. And I don't think the villagers are likely to lend us their healer. Gorgon Uni is the nearest help for him."

There was no point in standing about arguing. I made my way to the main door and peered out. Hewitt followed me, apparently done with the two at the altar.

I reached the door just as a shout rang out. "Wolves!" The call echoed across the mountain.

A quick peek told me I was wrong to expect everyone to rush back into the church for protection. Nay, they were careening down the hill.

I eyed the ladder. There was no one blocking the way, so up I went. The bell ringer was at the outer window. I joined him at the opening. He gave me plenty of room even though with only one arrow I was not much of a threat. My arsenal was woefully short of useful weapons.

Down in the valley, a flash of fur dashed from a merchant's shop to another building. Stone homes further from the center had even more activity. "The size of them!" I exclaimed. "Are the villagers thinking to fight them with bare hands?" I'd have run the other way or climbed a tree. Hmm. We really were very close to Wendal. And we had just freed a dragon.

I looked at the bell ringer. He was only a few years older than Hewitt.

"Hewitt!" I raced back to the ladder worried that Hewitt would be headed to the valley to chat up a wolf or three. Luckily, his face, starting to show streaks of dirt, looked up at me from below. "Hewitt. It's time for you to go back to mama."

To my intense relief, he nodded.

"Good. Let's be gone then."

Whether the dragon had sent the wolves to help or they had appeared on their own, I didn't care.

Unfortunately, as soon as I reached ground level, Brittany demanded my assistance with Irwin. I couldn't carry Hewitt and help with Irwin at the same time. "Hewitt, get going. Back to the horses, child. Go!"

Hewitt wasn't all that fast, but he did get moving. I grabbed Irwin's uninjured arm while Brittany took the one she had hurriedly patched.

"What is happening out there?" Brittany panted. Irwin's feet dragged as we limped out the door.

"Wolves in the village. If the creatures haven't run off the horses, we stand a chance."

Brittany halted. "Wol..ves? Are you crazy?"

"Yes." There was no other explanation for me being on this hill running after a four-year-old seer, half dragging a noble. "We had better make the horses before they do."

That got her feet churning, although she probably would have stayed in the church if the Anton warrior had actually died from her well-placed slingshot. If he regained consciousness she'd either have to kill him or he would kill all of us.

We fell twice. My knees bore the brunt of the damage because falling backwards while dragging a heavy person simply wasn't possible. Sweat drenched my face. By the time we got Irwin flung and tied over the supply horse, my legs were near collapse. I boosted Hewitt onto my pony, but even superbly trained as the mare was, when the wolf behind me growled, she reared back, eyes rolling.

"Go, Hewitt, go!" I flung the reins up to him, but my mount was a length away before my arm finished swinging. "Find—"

The wolf hit me hard from behind. My knees got off easy. This time I landed on my face.

Chapter 4

There were brief times when the rocking movement of travel almost woke me. The smell of wet fur reminded me of danger, but it was simply too much work to figure out. I faded each time, feeling cold on one side and warm on the other.

It was the pain in my knees that finally penetrated enough to make me open my eyes.

The dragon woman hovered over me, dabbing something vile smelling across my left leg.

"The leather didn't tear. It's just a scrape," I protested, having no real idea if I spoke the truth.

She slapped a cloth around my thigh and knee without bothering to refute my argument. I took in my surroundings, studying the sheer stone walls and a fireplace. It was not unlike Lonnie's tower room, except the castle walls were made of cut stone. The walls here were sheer rock.

The place was far richer than my simple dorm had been at Gorgon Uni. Thick tapestries, an ornate desk, and a fireplace with carvings directly in the stone decorated my current surroundings. The bed underneath me was as nice as anything my mother had sewn. "Wendal?" I asked.

Purple hooded eyes met mine. We judged each other again, much as the first time we had met; wary, distrusting, but curious enough to hold back the kill. Well, she had the advantage of a possible kill over me once again. I had stood little enough of a chance then and less of one now.

"Are you hungry?" she finally asked.

I took time to evaluate the question, pushing myself up on my elbows. My leather pants were gone. My tunic had been washed and given back to me. This was a good sign since I doubted they would have done my laundry if they intended to kill me immediately. In the soft glow of crystalline lanterns, a tray of covered dishes waited on a table near the bed.

"I think I am."

She nodded. "You'll need your strength in order to reverse your people's spell."

The glare in her eyes was not entirely human. The dragon lurked, alien and threatening. "Spell." My forehead wrinkled. "My people." I shook my head and then winced, feeling along my face. A rather large bump graced the bridge of my nose and part of my forehead. "I don't have any people, unless you mean my parents or my cousin. I am not of royal blood so I have no kingdom to trade."

She handed me bread. "You had better hope you can reverse the spell anyway."

With that ominous threat, she retreated, pushing the side table closer. There was more food and a goblet of water. I sat up and helped myself. While I chewed, she paced.

"I'm Zoe," I introduced myself. "Should I just shout 'hey you' or do you have another preference?"

"You may call me Lindis. Do you know how to reverse the spell on the ring?"

She was rather single-minded. It was more likely desperation than a normal dragon trait. "Probably not. I didn't create the spell and unwinding spells designed by another person often results in a shorter lifespan." I downed a rather huge chunk of cheese and nearly choked on it. A quickly chewed boiled egg cleared my throat. "Besides, I never had a chance to graduate Gorgon. I'm not even a half wizard, never mind a full one." That reminded me. "Did whoever leave me here bring my pack?"

She halted her pacing and pointed. Not only was my pack waiting by the fireplace on the floor, but the entire bag of Brittany's supplies rested there. I smiled. We had taken the supplies off to get Irwin on. When the wolves howled, Brittany had mounted, leaving me to settle Hewitt. The wolves had closed in, and the horses had decided Brittany had the right of it; they hadn't bothered to wait for me.

My smile disappeared. "Do you know if Hewitt—" I couldn't finish. Besides, the dragon woman was shaking her head. "The pack let them go. I told them I needed you. I hope I was not wrong."

"About needing me or not needing them?" My head throbbed, but it was time for answers.

"Both."

"Who are you that so many are dying to marry you?" I asked.

She blinked slowly, her eyes half shut while she studied me. If she had been full dragon, her tail might have lashed back and forth like that of a cat.

Her eyelids were purple. Having seen her a total of three times now, I finally realized the effect wasn't colored mica or bruises. When she went dragon, her scales were purple. Dragon. The most powerful of the rumored familiars, only of course, "familiars" was a false rumor. The dragons were human shifters. Or the other way around.

I sighed and touched the bump on my head. "You don't happen to have any willow tea, do you?"

"Hot or cold?"

"Hot."

She didn't respond other than to nod. I let it go. "I don't know much about Wendal," I said. "I'm going to guess that you're someone important and if you were to marry Irwin...I suppose he is the prince of Anton, although I didn't know that until I saw the warrior's colors. And Kal, the prince who called you to the castle in Birk, was also very interested in you."

She snorted. "You are very ignorant, aren't you?"

I shrugged. "I had no need to know the politics."

There was a knock at the door. She answered it and brought me a steaming pot of willow tea with a large cup and several plates of other herbs. Apparently dragons communicated some things without speech.

I poured the tea eagerly and sipped without adding any of the other herbs. "Oh, excellent." I needed the tea badly.

"Children are a rare thing in Wendal, especially in my family. I am unmarried and of age to mate. That has not happened in your lifetime. Or your cousin's or..." she tilted her head. "Even your king was not alive when the last dragon of mating age became available. And of course we hold sway in a rather large territory. Wendal is larger than the two kingdoms you already mentioned. If you include the two kingdoms north of yours and another one to the south of Birk, the area would be almost as large as Wendal." Her sneer was a barely held threat.

"So you're next in line for the throne here?"

One dark eyebrow rose. "We don't have a throne, but yes, we dragons have considerable influence. It's an earned right and granted mainly because of our abilities and long lives, but also because we leave well enough alone when it comes to business not our own."

"But if you married someone from another kingdom, what would it mean?"

Fire burned behind her eyes. "Nothing, unless they controlled me."

"Cousin Lonnie could not have controlled you from that pentagram he drew," I assured her. "I'm still not certain what he was trying to accomplish. How could they have forced you to marry Kal? And what would that have meant?"

Her fists clenched. "It's possible that my clan would want me back. They might be convinced to sacrifice some territory. Or meet other demands."

I nodded. "Ah, royalty and the usual games. Give up everything, and you can sort of have her back because we won't kill her. Let us move a few people into your castle and eat all your food."

"That is overly simplified." The eyebrow quirked and she nodded. "But rather accurate. I think you left off the part where eventually they'd want to enslave our abilities, our children and our children's children. And in the unlikely case that I might bear a child that did not die, that would up the ante if my clan didn't just burn your cities to the ground to get us back." She stalked closer. "Is it really possible you did not know who I am?"

"Apparently. Dragons are not of high concern to one of my low stature. I've only heard rumors of Wendal. Until now I didn't know anyone who had actually been here."

"That cousin of yours is in a position of power. He must have known!"

"I doubt it. Cousin Lonnie was apprenticed to the castle wizard only three years ago. He became the wizard because the previous wizard died. In fact, I am fairly certain Lonnie is the reason the castle wizard inhaled a rather untimely fire spell and cooked from the inside out."

"Your cousin killed him to gain his spot?"

"Not so much. Lonnie doesn't do much on purpose, but Lonnie was likely the reason for the accident. Near as I can tell, the wizard asked for a certain ingredient. Lonnie is lazy. He either got the jars mixed up or he decided on his own that since they were out of one ingredient, the other would do. And being Lonnie, he didn't mention this to the wizard."

She held up one long finger that in the low light resembled a talon. "Where do you fit in?"

"I'm his cousin and not an idiot. My mother provided me with enough magical training to keep him out of trouble, at least until he called you. The king wouldn't accept a female wizard, so there was no chance of me actually holding the position. I shipped myself off to Gorgon Uni to gain an education and hopefully find a spot in another territory or kingdom. The northern kingdoms are rumored to have at least two female mages. But then, the rumors about Wendal aren't all true either."

"Can you reverse the spell in the ring?" she hissed.

"You'd better let me look at it. But while I'm doing that, will you please tell me what happened? Because I'm damned tired of running around trying to figure it out."

She refused to take the ring off, but she offered me her cold and nearly blue digits. The glyphs around the blue stone were a complete mystery to me, but I separated each into my brain. I traced a couple on the table, not completing them. I didn't recognize a single one, not even broken into parts.

"When your cousin's spell failed to hold me, the next breach was worse," she said.

I turned her hand palm up to study the band. "There are words or glyphs on the inside of the band, aren't there? Yes, there would have to be because it's the only part that touches you."

"And when it is not touching me, I cannot become what I am meant to be. My heritage was taken from me in a single moment." Her hand shook. "I had to follow the ring. The pain of the separation from my dragon was unbearable." Her voice faded to a smoky whisper.

"They trapped your dragon in the ring. Bound it somehow to the stone. I need to see the words on the inside of the band."

"No!"

"You can keep your hand on it. I'm not exactly about to hop out the door and escape."

"Your cousin could call you away like he did me."

Hysteria bubbled in my throat. "No, actually he cannot. I made sure of that a long time ago."

She slid the ring off her finger and let it rest on her open palm. Her other hand gripped my neck with claws. "You won't live to speak if you go."

"Right." I bent over the ring. "I need more light."

Once we were settled with a glowing crystalline lamp nearby, I studied the glyphs. Thanks to Lonnie, I recognized the symbol for binding. If not for him, it might have been years and another mage-school before I ever encountered it. Since he had called Lindis, the dragon symbol was easy enough to recognize. I flipped it back to see the top, but there was simply nothing there that was recognizable.

I sat back. "Okay. You can put it back on."

"Can you reverse it?"

I didn't meet her eyes. "Not a chance." I was truly sorry. "I can't read it. The inside is a binding for your dragon. When you are touching the ring, you and the dragon are one. But the dragon is bound to the ring somehow."

"Who can help me?"

"Who spelled the ring?" I countered.

"One of yours," she hissed. "No one here works mage magic. We've had no need for it."

I frowned. "What of the crystalline mage lanterns?" I pointed to the one on the table.

She shrugged. "We trade with your people. We supply crystals that are of no use to us and your mages fire them up. We often trade food supplies, especially near the border. It's only right since ofttimes we hunt across the border. We need the food supplies and we're happy to sell some...less desirable parts back since it is their territory after all." Her eyes glinted with humor at putting one over on her neighbors, but then she turned more serious. "Maybe we can trade you for a more powerful mage."

"I told you. I'm a nobody. If you tried to trade for me, it would take weeks for the king to figure out who I am, if he cared to ask. Most likely he would merely laugh. Worst case, he'd attempt to steal you away again, although I'm still not certain he was responsible for Lonnie and Kal's attempt."

"What of your cousin? Would he bargain for you?"

A self-deprecating smile took over my face. "He'd probably like me back, but only to save himself the trouble of learning his own spells. That's if he hasn't been thrown out of the castle entirely." My birds hadn't informed me of his fall from grace, but news hadn't been that easy to obtain in Gorgon.

Her fingers clenched around the ring.

"Who spelled it?" I asked. "Do you know?"

"Explain to me the person I need. I will bring her here."

Her despair was a difficult thing to behold. Animals had always tugged at my heartstrings and their hearts spoke often in my mind. Her desperation was all human, but the beat of her emotion was like that of a suffering animal. It pained me. "You must have some idea who did this to you. Whoever it was came close."

"Why not your cousin or your prince? They were close to me!"

"In your dragon form?"

She looked up, confused. "I am always dragon."

I pointed to the ring. "The gem. Something of dragon is locked inside that stone." I didn't have to read the glyphs to know that much. "A binding always uses hair, skin..." I stopped and regrouped. "Scales.

Something of your dragon. Did those seeking your hand in marriage visit? Did you turn them down in person?"

She snorted. "They wouldn't dare approach. They have nothing to offer. And I only take audience with humans in human form. They are ignorant of dragon ways."

A knock interrupted what could have become a tirade. Her eyes flashed, but it was unclear whether this was a new anger or the old one. She eyed me as though weighing my fate. It was a long moment before she opened the door.

Chapter 5

The visitor was a large man, though most of it was height. He moved with a smooth grace that had me assuming he was dragon also. Where Lindis' pace was a darting quickness that my eyes sometimes failed to track, his glide had him well inside the room before I realized he had done more than step inside.

"Derrick," she greeted him as if his name was a curse.

"It's late," he said.

Lindis hissed.

He ignored the threat to study me with large brown eyes that were flecked with gold. His hair was a dark gray decorated with lighter silver and brown streaks, a range of colors that was probably impossible to achieve without magic. Or...it was the eyes and the voice that gave him away. "Wolf!"

His surprise was only an instant, but his glance at Lindis told me it had been real. Lindis didn't react to my announcement other than to blink calmly.

He moved closer to me. "You've stalled past reason, Lindis. She comes with me now." It was not a suggestion or plea, but his voice was tainted with some regret.

"I am not finished with her."

His eyes scanned me, missing nothing. I forced my clenched fists and shoulders to relax. I wished heartily for a tree to climb. When I assessed the bed canopy, his lips lifted, but only in a half smile. "It would do you little good here and now," he said.

"Why do I have to go with the wolves?" I asked Lindis.

"I am crippled."

"You can change as long as you have the ring."

She gave me the slow dragon glare. "Twice I have been compromised. Once I was returned and not even under my own power, thanks to you." Her voice was a cross between a snarl and a low growl. "The second time, I had no choice but to follow the call. I was completely compelled until I retrieved the ring." Her fisted hand suddenly sported sharp talons. Her fingers were clenched so tightly, a drop of blood cascaded onto the floor.

The wolf sniffed as the smell of blood reached him. I had to make do with my eyes.

"Now that I consider the situation properly, getting the ring back was also your doing. I cannot be trusted to guard you until we find a way to erase the threat. If I am compromised, Wendal is at risk. Derrick has first right to be your guard because he brought you here even though it was at my request." Her talons eased back. "You need to learn quickly, human. There are many here who don't trust you, and if they find you cannot help me, your time with us will be short."

"Don't threaten her," Derrick intervened. "She didn't come here looking for trouble."

Lindis ignored him in favor of hounding me. "Can you learn this spell or must I find another?"

"You need a full mage," I advised. "And even then, I'm not sure it can be done. Reversing someone else's spell—"

"You reversed spells easily once before!"

It took me a moment to follow her reasoning. "Lonnie learned much about spells from me. The rest he learned from the wizard, but in order to work them he had to show me the texts. I helped him often enough that undoing any of his is not that difficult. And I know he did not spell that ring." I shook my head. "He hasn't half the talent needed. Someone had a piece of you. And if they did not come here to get it, it was taken to them."

The wolf tilted his head. "You might be of use yet," he said.

Lindis' eyes flared when he reached the bed in a single motion.

He blocked out most of the room by towering over me. "Come."

It didn't seem like the best idea. "I need my pants. And my pack. And—"

He scooped me up. I panicked. Power abused, especially on those assumed to have none was a fact I lived with, but it was not the first time I had needed to escape it. My smallest backup crystals were woven into my tunic; just another part of the design. Without hesitation, I gripped one and uttered the word of power.

The world exploded in a rash of color, the yellow pulse pushing the wolf away from me. I landed half across the bed, but I was no stranger to a physical fight either. I rolled forward easily, taking myself to my pack. It was not much protection, but it was all I had. There was nowhere to run. I backed to the flames, coming close enough to nearly set myself on fire. My pack in front of me wasn't much of a barrier.

The wolf was on his feet snarling and halfway to me when Lindis stepped between us.

"Methinks you might not want to treat her so much as a cub," she said.

Lindis kept her eyes on him, which gave me time to retrieve my dagger from my boot. Not that it would help much. The wolf was nearly twice my size and faster than anyone I had ever seen, unless I counted Lindis.

The low snarl from behind Lindis raised my fear another notch. "Your clan has agreed that you are not fit to be her guardian. If a mage is to be here, she is not going to live unguarded to compromise Wendal more than it already is. If she is the means to freeing you, she must be safe where she cannot steal away or be stolen away if thieves come to try and marry you off again."

Instead of the despair of before, Lindis eased sideways and graced him with the haughty look of one who knows she could win in a fight. She may have forgotten herself momentarily but even controlled by a ring, inside and out, she was a dragon. "If she kills you, you won't be much of a guardian. If you kill her, what good is she? You forget yourself." Her voice was steel, tinted with the smoke of a barely banked fire. "Do you really think a human who rescued a dragon twice is someone to cart off over your shoulder?"

His jaw ticked, and he eyed me rather more carefully than before. I let the pack fall, revealing the dagger in my other hand. It wasn't much of a threat. I had seen Lindis with a sword. I had seen this guy as a wolf. My only advantage was that they didn't know me. That wasn't enough to make us even, but it was enough to warrant caution on their part.

"It's always better to walk under my own steam." I straightened from my fighting stance. "I'll get dressed and go." It wasn't as if there was a real choice, but pretending made me feel better.

Derrick straightened his own defensive posture, but didn't leave.

"Could you give me some privacy?"

His bushy eyebrows frowned.

Lindis held up a hand. "She's not a cub."

"I don't relish tracking out of here with her full of weapons I know nothing about!"

"I'm already armed," I pointed out. "So you already don't know about them. Adding to them isn't going to make any difference." It actually would, but he didn't need to know that.

With a snarl, he turned around. My hearing wasn't all that great, but my ability for animal empathy filled in the grunts and teeth gnashing. He was angry at being shown up by a tiny human female. His alpha nature longed to slap me down. Yeah, well. Lots of people had that reaction. Lonnie had tried more than once with a spell, which is why I was heavily armed against him.

After donning my pants, I fingered the spent crystal. I had my larger crystal in my pocket now and still had two others.

"Are you done yet?" Derrick snapped.

"I'm curling my hair." It was a lie that had him turning fast in disbelief. I wrinkled my nose to keep from grinning outright. My mouth did not seem to care much about survival.

Lindis grinned for me, but she was not facing the wolf.

Using up one of my only weapons was probably not wise, but Lindis had never harmed me despite multiple opportunities. "Must we leave right this second? So long as you're here guarding me, I mean?" I asked the wolf. It was late to pretend deference, but maybe not too late.

He crossed his arms, probably to keep from shaking me. "You're dressed. You are not going to curl your hair."

I saved my attention for Lindis. "I can spell a crystal to protect you from Lonnie." I chewed my lip. "It will ward against the spell he used to call you. That way he can't do it again. Even if Prince Kal gets any bright ideas to hire a smarter wizard, he wouldn't be able to use the spell on you."

"How long?" Derrick asked on a sigh.

"Not long. Maybe ten minutes."

Lindis stepped closer to me. "Why is there a problem I sense?"

There was indeed. "I work with crystals. I'm trying to think of a way that you wouldn't have to wear it. I could ward this room, but you can't take the ward with you unless it's stored in something like the crystal. I could tie the spell to metal, but unless you want to carry the fire poker around, I don't have anything else to tie it to."

Her head lifted back, tense.

"Yeah, I didn't figure you'd like being saddled with another crystal. I can start with the room."

"Which still leaves me bound. The restrictions get tighter and tighter. My movement is already limited. Will your cousin try this spell again?"

"Lonnie isn't that bright."

"I would rather crush you like a bug than accept another tie."

"It isn't a tie. You're not bound to carry it. You can leave it whenever you choose."

Derrick made a low noise in the back of his throat, maybe a stifled snort.

"My choices were taken from me quite some time ago," Lindis growled softly.

In the end, Derrick agreed to wait. I used the orange crystal even though it was my favorite. It was fully charged with the power and heat from a fire. The crystal was a potent weapon, one that could not only set fire to an opponent, but myself as well if I wasn't careful. Mostly I used it to start a cooking fire when traveling.

Since I needed every weapon possible and had already used up my yellow, I set the yellow in the fireplace to recharge while I used the orange to ward the room. Derrick and Lindis didn't need to know one crystal was recharging while I used up the other.

Surreptitiously, I drew the glyphs of the spell around the yellow. The glyphs would draw the heat as power into the crystal for later use.

For the orange, I pulled bare bits of trapped power off of it as I marked the room with the glyphs that would ward it specifically from Lonnie and from the spell he had used. I remembered all of the glyphs he had used. Memorizing spells had been drummed into me early and soaking up any spells Lonnie used was second nature.

Even tapping into the crystal lightly, it was almost spent by the time I finished the room. Lindis might feel the walls were closing in on her, but the room was huge by any normal human standards.

"I feel no different," Lindis complained warily.

"It's been longer than ten minutes," was Derrick's observation.

"Sorry," I said to him. "I'm having trouble with my knees." Normally, I'd have squatted by the lowest edges of the room and then tied it all to a point in the ceiling center, but every time I crouched, I had to sit flat because one knee was still swollen and the other had a scrape that split open the first time I knelt down. My head was starting to seriously hurt again too.

"Can this ward be erased?" Lindis asked.

I nodded. "Yes, but not by the maids. It's an energy field, not a physical one."

She came over to the wall and sniffed. "Your cousin had a physical drawing."

Derrick followed and breathed deeply.

"Lonnie always does. He has trouble seeing the energy fields he draws so he always uses sand or coal pencils. He has to go back and erase areas constantly too. Energy lines are harder to see and to reassemble if they are disrupted. I can see my own, but it's impossible to see the fields from other mages unless they draw them in ashes or sand as Lonnie does."

I sat on the edge of the bed with a tired sigh. There was still tea so I helped myself to it and some more bread.

"Do you require more food?" Lindis asked.

I shook my head. "No. Setting the crystal for you will be easier." The only problem was that the orange was spent. I'd have to use the refueled yellow and that depressed me. I had not intended to give up two crystals. The small blue and a large white would be my only remaining sources of defense. I wasn't up to my normal speed either. In fact, sitting down made me realize just how hard it was going to be to get started again. I was tapped out and short two crystals because no way did I have the energy to reset the orange one that had powered the ward.

I started to retrieve the yellow from the fire, but in truth, dizziness was fast taking over. My hand shook. If I expended my energy to set the yellow crystal to protect Lindis, I'd fall flat into the fire. "Are you going to stay in this room for a while?" I asked.

She shrugged. "It is night. I might fly. I might not. Why?"

If she stayed here until I rested, things would be vastly easier, but who knew whether Derrick intended to ever let me come back? Who knew if I'd even be alive tomorrow?

I stared into the flames, letting them soothe me. My own tiredness had nearly hypnotized me when it finally occurred to me that Lindis was a dragon. Not everyone could perform magic, but a dragon? Why not? She might even know how already and if not, warding glyphs were easy enough to learn.

"Okay," I said. "You set the yellow one." If she couldn't set this thing herself, she was out of luck, because I was completely spent.

"I am not a mage. There are no mages in Wendal."

I blinked. "How can there be none?"

"None."

"But...you threw a bolt of magic large enough to toast me dead when Lonnie called you!"

She laughed. "That was not a magic bolt, that was dragon fire. Just because I was in human form didn't mean I was without dragon fire. I can throw fire balls from a long distance, and I rarely miss. You are lucky I was off-balance, and your cousin's panic warned you."

"Have you ever tried to set your own spells?" Desperation colored my voice. If she couldn't do it, we were at a stalemate. I simply didn't have the energy.

"If I could work spells, wouldn't I know? Mages are from your side of the border. No one here does magic."

"That's not a reason. You're a shifter. You go across the border. And I came here, and while I'm not a mage, I'm mage material. I just worked magic so it works here." I shrugged. "Maybe you just need training. Pick a word. A gesture. Something that no one else is likely to notice. You're going to want to put your energy or emotion into it. You can't just say the word, you have to tie it to your inner self. If you use anger to complete it, you'll need anger to release it. It doesn't have to be the same word to set it and activate it, but you have to remember the difference." I gave her the quick version of the long lecture that Lonnie received on a regular basis. "And you'll want to remember not to use the word of power at the wrong time or you'll be releasing the wards and putting them back up by accident. Let me show you what you're activating."

I provided a very quick and dirty tour of the dragon symbol. "By itself, this one just conjures illusionary baby dragons. They're a magical representation, but they can still breathe fire if there's enough energy backing them because the fire glyph is included." I drew the other two lines I had learned from Lonnie's transportation spell. "This symbol adds a human female, which makes it a reference to a human dragon, which is what you are. Other symbols can be used, but you must include the one for a human girl because if you became separated from your ring, I'm not sure having the dragon alone would stop the spell."

She hissed.

I ignored the threat. "Are you ready? When you are, here is what you draw to close the spell. Then when the crystal has cooled from the fire, you retrieve it."

"You touched the other crystal while you worked," she said.

"It wasn't hot from the fire."

Her hooded eyes watched the flames much as mine had done earlier. Finally, she reached into the flames for the crystal, hissed an unrepeatable and unintelligible noise of triumph and set the last line.

I felt the link snap into place. This time, she felt it too. She froze, sensing the wards, feeling them. For me, they were a spark of light with a weight, not heavy and not unpleasant, almost like a butterfly. If I didn't think about them, I didn't even know they were there, but if I watched the wards, they wafted around me like the lightest of breezes.

"It is different than what you did before." It was a question and a statement.

"I should have had you set the ward for your room, but it's true that not everyone can be trained to do magic. Why aren't people from Wendal trained? You obviously could be." I scooted back, watching while she pulled the crystal out of the fire. Her hand was completely uninjured from the flames. Fire and dragons went well together. I had chosen the right type of energy for her by accident.

"Magic isn't practiced here." She frowned, her attention on the crystal. "We have no real need. I have certainly never tried." She finally faced me, her glare at full force. "If harm comes to me from this rock—"

"You can drop the wards at any time," I said. "Try it. You can reset them too. Eventually I'll have to recharge the crystal using the energy from the fire, but it will last a long while if nothing hits the wards." I gave her a stern warning on not using her own energy to shore up the spell. "Lonnie tries that all the time because he does spells on the fly. It's the reason a lot of his spells fail. He'll kill himself one day overextending himself. When the energy runs low in the crystal, I'll show you how to redo it."

"Show me now!"

Derrick was out of patience. "We've wasted enough time. It's been an hour since she started. Do it later. My pack grows restless with the delay. They want reassurances that you will abide by the agreement, and allow us to keep her safe."

It was for the better that he intervened. I didn't have any teaching left in me. In fact, armed or not, I probably couldn't set off another of my protection crystals if my life depended upon it. Derrick was quite safe from me, if he had ever been in any danger at all.

It was plain from the glint in his eyes that he suspected my state of fatigue. "Do you wish me to carry you out of here, or will you go under your own power?"

I ground my teeth. Two deep breaths and I made it to my feet, barely swaying. Staying upright might not have happened had he not put his hand possessively on my arm.

Lindis did not protest this time. She fingered her gold necklace for a moment. When her hand came away, the yellow crystal was threaded neatly along the loop. I stared at it while Lindis handed the supply pack and my pack to Derrick. "This is not over."

"No," he agreed. "Far from it." He nearly dragged me over with his first long stride to the door. He gave an impatient sigh, but backed up a step and let me take shorter ones.

From his grumbling, I gathered patience would be the death of him.

Chapter 6

I managed fine in the hallways and great stone corridors of the dragon's lair, but when we reached the outer edge, it became immediately clear that Lindis and her clan lived in a vast castle that was carved straight into a stone cliff.

Lindis argued with Derrick over whether we would walk down under our own power or she would fly us. I dozed against the side of the wall, which may have been the deciding factor.

She finally flew both of us down from the cliff, one at a time. It was that or let Derrick lower me through a complicated inner tunnel that was more footholds in stone than a stairway. Derrick was quite gleeful in explaining that a rope was required in several spots. He was just launching into a harrowing description of the false maze of tunnels when Lindis changed.

She wasted no words flipping me up onto her back. The dizziness never had a chance to clear before she glided to the ground and dumped me like a sack of supplies.

She returned in moments with Derrick. He rode rather more gracefully than I had and dismounted better too. It seemed a lot of trouble to get up from the dirt, but I doubted our final destination was the middle of a forest between four trees. Then again, he was a wolf. Maybe he bedded down wherever he landed. At the moment, it didn't seem like a terrible idea, although the damp ground was seeping into my pants. It was also broad daylight, somewhere around midmorning if I had to guess.

With a tired sigh, I stood.

He took my arm. It was impossible not to lean against him because I swayed before finding my balance. "It would be easier to carry you," he said wryly.

I had no reply, and unless I sleep-walked, he must have carried me part of the time because when I woke up, we were in front of a pleasant stone house with stout wooden shutters. Trees grew right up to its base. The sound and smell of a nearby brook merged with the twittering of birds and sigh of the wind through the maples, oaks and vines of the forest.

Derrick opened the door and swept his arm inside. "After you, cub."

I stumbled through the door and found the first chair. The expected pack of wolves was nowhere to be seen. The quiet told me we were still alone. A bed, thick with blankets, was on one end of the cottage. The table and chairs were close to a fireplace with banked coals. The kitchen area looked well-stocked; dried goods hung from the rafters.

I yawned so hard my jaw cracked. "Where are the others? Your pack?"

He strode past me without answering. My heart felt the first stirrings of panic. There was no one to protect me from his rage should he decide he was done with me. I doubted any lingering threat from Lindis would stop him from doing as he saw fit.

There was only one thing I really wanted to know before I died. "Did Hewitt make it?"

He spun in surprise. I realized he had been reviving the kitchen stove, not sharpening a knife for my throat. "Hewitt?" he parroted.

"The...little boy. On the horse. Right before you hit me."

He was so still, he might not have been breathing. "You are old enough for a cub of your own, aren't you? He was yours?"

How to answer that? If I said yes, was he more likely to be sympathetic? But if he thought I longed to find my child, he might dangle it as an incentive to coerce me to cooperate. If I said no, he wouldn't be able to use Hewitt as leverage against me. I was too tired to figure out the most advantageous response.

He took my silence as an answer. "He and the other two on the horses ran free." He disappeared out a back door. When he returned, he carried an alarmingly large slab of meat, some bread and eggs. He worked at the stove while I dozed, nearly senseless.

When the supper, or by my best guess—noon meal—was ready, he served it on tin plates. The grilled meat he heaped on my plate was enough for four of me. I ate a slice, two eggs and was thrilled he had heated water. There was no tea, but the water was nicely warm.

"The pack is scattered about," he told me between bites of food. "We live free, much like the dragons, although their lair is interwoven with tunnels. Their towers are not unlike the forest is for us; they're a non-intrusive lot, at least they were until you people interfered.

"I didn't interfere. I was just there."

"Lindis says that was a good thing, although I didn't think she liked you until today."

"I didn't like her much either." Then I shrugged. "Well, really I had nothing against her other than she showed up in a bad place a couple of times."

"Through no fault of her own."

"Not mine either." With the food and the restful walk that was a dim dream, I felt much better.

"How old is your cub?"

Uncomfortable, I dropped my gaze. "Four."

"His father will come looking for you."

Ah, that explained his interest. He was worried about an attack or me being stolen away before I could help Lindis. I pulled on my braid. If I said yes, would he attempt to head off any rescuers? And what would happen when no one came?

"You traveled alone that first time when I saw you in the tree."

Uh-oh. He had a good memory, and it wouldn't take much to arrange the pieces and find some missing. "Uh-huh." I took a sip of my now cool water.

"Where was your cub?" His hand snaked out and captured my wrist.

I tensed. He knew what my crystals could do, but he also now had an idea of how they worked. If I made a grab for one, as fast as he moved, he'd be able to stop me.

"Do you think he made it back to Gorgon University?" I asked.

He held me more with his eyes than his giant hand. "Hopefully not. Gorgon had a very nasty fire the night after we took you. Couple of the pack checked it out, but not many of your people made it out."

I blinked. "Brittany? Did she make it back?" Then again, Brittany might not have headed to Gorgon. But Hewitt... "Fire." Hewitt had predicted the fire! What had Hewitt said? Something about a fire and his mother coming for him. I didn't remember his words exactly, but maybe his mother was alive. And if she had been out looking, her husband, the Mage-Master Alcen, would have been out searching too. Probably. Hopefully, Hewitt knew how to find his mother after he escaped from the wolves. Not that the wolves had been interested in him.

Derrick released my wrist. "You are even more interesting than Lindis indicated. Are you going to finish your meat?"

My eyes widened. "Are you crazy? I can't eat all that unless we dry it as jerky and save it for later." I was not one to waste food. Neither, apparently, was he. Despite having eaten nearly all of a back quarter of the deer meat, he helped himself to my leftovers.

Chapter 7

Mother and Father would be worried sick, especially once news of the fire at Gorgon reached them. Normally a sparrow or finch wouldn't travel far this time of year; the sparrows tended to stay in a very small territory. But with the fire at Gorgon, it was possible some birds might relocate and be able to carry messages. It was also possible Mother would pack her bags and come check the fire for herself, whether Father approved or not. Which meant they would both show up where I was not.

Derrick had a water pump in the kitchen. In the bathing room, he had a shower of the type that wasn't all that common. Water was stored along the back of the stove and a hand pump in the bathroom pulled the hot water from there. It was way better than the cold pump at the school.

With the nice indoor features, getting cleaned up was wonderful, but it eliminated every possible excuse for going outside alone. Getting a message out via birds was proving difficult. Maybe I could sneak out after dark.

Finished with my bathing, I sat back at the table. "Are there bats here?" They had larger territories than birds, but maybe they were dragon fare or rare. A nighthawk...no, probably wouldn't go all the way to Central. By my very bad estimate, I was at least a day's walk into Wendal. But I had traveled by wolf, not man, and I was pretty sure wolf was faster. Central was a long way to convince a bat to carry a message.

Derrick scratched his ear. He contemplated the wash bucket, which was now empty of the dirty dishes. Finally he folded his arms over his chest. "I cannot think of a single reason for you to ask that. And I've given it due consideration. Is this a magic spell thing?"

He already knew more than enough about my spells. If I hadn't been so tired, the bat thing wouldn't have slipped out.

"I need sleep." I pillowed my head on my arms. "Never mind. I'll tell you in the morning." A bald-faced lie if there ever was one.

"Use the blankets. I'll run the perimeter. I won't need the bed. It's only midday, but I've traveled as much as you have. An afternoon to catch up on sleep is a good idea."

Well, that was one night's—day's—rest solved. And if he was outside checking things, it was probably not a good idea for me to go in search of bats or birds to play messenger.

He didn't have to offer the bed twice. Tired as I was, if he decided to take advantage of me, I probably wouldn't even notice.

I half woke when he returned, wolf, as promised. Sleepily I noted that his door handle lever opened by pushing down, something he could easily manage with a paw. Clever. I stared into yellow wolf eyes long enough for my heart to beat faster. Derrick was all wolf; wary, distrusting and much like his human counterpart except that it was almost easier to read him as a wolf.

"Nice doggie," I joked, setting my heart tripping even faster. He could probably hear the nervous pattering. The fur on the back of his neck ruffled straight up and he bared his teeth, but he didn't mean it. I smiled, relieved. "'Night." I was lucky he didn't nip my ankles.

He growled an empty grumble at my lack of respect. With a contented roll of his tongue, he dropped in front of the door.

I fell asleep halfway back to the pillow.

Chapter 8

I woke up hours later, but felt less battered than I had in days. Very late day sunlight streamed through the open shutters. Derrick was not inside. I jumped up from the blankets and clutched my crystals through the special pockets sewn in my tunic. The fire in the stove was the warmest, so I removed one of the cast iron plates, dropped the spent orange crystal into the coals, and made sure the log caught properly before putting the lid back on. Tracing the glyphs that would pull the heat into the crystal took me only a minute. Derrick wouldn't likely notice the crystal there in the ashes. Why would he even look at anything closely in there?

I scurried to the bath, longing for a tub, but thrilled with the shower. The water was not quite as hot as it had been for my earlier washing, but still a blessing.

Fully refreshed, I wandered out back to find the cellar. The day would turn to dusk in less than an hour. I had slept the entire afternoon, but there was just enough time for an important chore. The happy chirping of birds greeted my eager ears. "Oh, good."

I whistled a quick melody, but getting in a chirp edgewise with sparrows or finches was tricky. Hmm. Wandering further without my pack and dagger would be foolhardy.

I darted back inside to sheath my dagger in my boot. Brittany's supply pack yielded some apples probably meant for the horses, but good enough for me. I also nabbed a handful of grain. Oh, this was luck, indeed.

The birds remained undisturbed by a returning wolf, so I greeted them again and chirped my way into the trees. The source of the eggs appeared first, in the form of two very large chickens pecking through the first set of trees. With luck, finding their nests shouldn't be too difficult.

"Afternoon, hens. Are there many of you?" Chickens were the least intelligent of the birds, but it never paid to ignore them even though they showed little enough interest in me.

The finches were not very friendly either, nor did they seem particularly impressed when I told them I was fine. Messenger birds they were not, but if someone asked them, they would have a sense of my message. It was going to take time to get word back to Mother that I was safe and had not been hurt when Gorgon went up in flames.

I asked about the smoke. My question caused one of the finches to twitter nervously. She knew of the fire. "If someone near the place of smoke asks about me, tell them I am fine." I tossed the grain on the ground near the bushes where the females were fighting over the nectar or bugs in the flowers. I asked about a small child and a mage, but the birds had no reason to be interested in such. I sighed, feeling lonely and lost. A much more intelligent source was required in order to glean any important information. If I needed dragon news or wolf news these four could probably help me, but that wasn't particularly helpful. "Remember, I am fine," I repeated. "And I am in Wendal."

"Do the finches care?"

My hearing was good, but I had expected the birds to be wary of the wolf and warn me if he approached. My startled yelp sent them flying where his voice had not. I spun from the empty bush and found Derrick behind me in the shadow of a tree.

"Are you so lonely you talk to the birds? Or do you tell your story to everyone?"

I dusted my hands off against my pants. "I was hoping they'd tell me where the cellar was. Or the chickens' nest."

"Yes, the finches are exactly who I would ask first."

"Why do they stay here? And the chickens too. Don't they smell wolf?"

His eyes narrowed. "Are you insulting me again?"

Since I wasn't certain when the first time might have been, I shrugged. "Apparently. Although I'm not really sure how."

"The nice doggie doesn't chase the chickens. I am not only wolf. The eggs are a good source of protein, reliable and easy. Just like they are for you."

I smiled, but his posture told me he was truly insulted. "I was tired. And teasing. Do not get worked up over it." I sighed. "As for the birds and the chickens, human or wolf, you must feed them or they'd be more than half wild. That is good. I'd have thought you would be more interested in the chickens for the meat, and that would have made them wary of you."

He growled.

"Oh, stop it. You are a wolf. Why wouldn't you eat the meat?"

"You really are as ignorant as Lindis promised, aren't you? It is not wise to go around calling people here animals."

"Apparently not, but I don't regard it as an insult." I slapped my hands against my thighs in frustration. "You don't eat chicken? I eat chicken. Chicken sausage. Roasted and stuffed is my favorite."

"It makes more sense to use the free roaming chickens for eggs than a single meal. We are not unintelligent beasts."

"Of course not." The finches were no longer very close, but when they stopped twittering entirely, even in the midst of our argument, the cessation of tweets alerted me. The finches had just fled from this direction. What had they encountered that was worse?

I reached for my crystal and moved fast towards Derrick. This was his glen, and he told Lindis he'd keep me safe. The birds' sudden silence indicated danger, whether they meant to warn me or not.

The one thing I hadn't thought of when spelling the crystals to help Lindis was that people might come here to find her instead of trying to kidnap her elsewhere. Protecting myself from visitors hadn't occurred to me either, because who in their right mind would be interested in me?

Chapter 9

The birds were either very sensitive to magic or to displaced air. Unfortunately, their warning silence did not come soon enough. I never made it to Derrick.

Three steps in his direction, I hit a sudden wall of human flesh. "Oof."

Cousin Lonnie dropped directly in front of me, taking the brunt of impact as I rushed forward. He tumbled backwards, his arms circling me. He hit much harder than I did.

"Gotcha," he cried.

"You idiot! You—" He took two deep breaths while I wasted time sputtering. His lungs expanded a third time, and his lips moved in nearly slow motion. I knew the word he would utter.

"No!" I sucked in a desperate breath, ready to stop him, but before I could utter the word, a solid weight landed on top of me, smashing me speechless. All of the air rushed out of my lungs in an unintelligible squawk.

The world went strangely dark. My stomach lurched. My head detached from my body for a moment. All too fast we landed.

"Mooof." I was sandwiched much the same on the other end with Lonnie under me and Derrick on top. Lonnie was not a real threat when he was at his best. He couldn't use a sword to save his life, and if he had wanted me dead, he wouldn't have bothered to suck me back to Central. I was *not* going to come back to Central and be his unpaid lackey, I was not!

Lonnie took the brunt of the landing against the cold stone floor of the castle. My weight would not have been enough to trouble him, but with Derrick included, his face reddened as he gasped for air.

I grabbed his white locks in my free hand and screamed, "I'm going to skewer you on a poker!" I slammed his head against the floor. "If you so much as speak a single word, I swear I will kill you!" My other arm was trapped between us, holding the crystal I had reached for when the birds went silent. With Derrick's heavy weight on top of me, I had no leverage.

"Rats in a dungeon full of dung." The castle tower room was dark, but I could see the outlines of the pentagram around us. "Don't move, Derrick. Don't even wiggle." Derrick was much taller than Lonnie and certainly taller than me. If his feet were outside the diagram we could be trapped here.

"You've got to help me," Lonnie moaned.

The only other object inside the pentagram was a book. The thick leather-bound text rested open to the page Lonnie had last been using. A book. A text on calling. And if it was the same as the one he had used for Lindis, it might well be a book that contained spells for binding too.

I released my hold on Lonnie's hair and wrapped my hand around the pages I could reach.

"If you don't help me, they'll put me in the dungeon!" Lonnie cried.

"Derrick, don't you dare let go of me. If you value your life, hold me tight and don't even think about letting go. I mean it." Nabbing one corner of the book, I scooted it closer. As I pulled it, inch by inch, the door to the tower room burst open, slamming against the stone wall. Shouts mingled with the sounds of swords leaving their scabbards. Without thinking twice, I clutched the pages and uttered Lonnie's word of power to redo the spell he had done.

He opened his mouth, probably to utter the opposite, but no way was he going to win this one. I couldn't feel my own head, but did my best to slam the book against his mouth. I pressed my weight down and held on despite my stomach lurching again. So soon after the first upset, I thought for certain I'd lose my lunch, but it was over quickly.

The act of crashing back in Wendal put a permanent dent in Lonnie's lips. As a bonus, his head smacked the ground so hard it rendered him unconscious. It was quite possibly the best thing that had happened to me in days.

Derrick had one arm wrapped firmly around my waist. The other came in high across my breasts. As soon as he smelled familiar loam, he rolled with me, taking my unresisting form away from cousin Lonnie. After two full rolls, it was a relief to be on top of him rather than squished underneath.

Derrick sat up without letting me go. I clutched the book and my spent crystal and leaned back against his chest, glad to be safe from whatever swords had been about to come after Lonnie.

"Can I assume this is not your beloved husband come to rescue you?"

"You don't miss a thing." I took a grateful breath. "You can let me go now."

"Hmm." His head rested atop mine. "But my life depends on holding you, if I recall correctly." His deep whisper sent shivers down my spine. My toes tingled, probably from residual magic. My arms felt strangely weightless, but I was safe. Completely safe. I took another deep breath. At the same time, Derrick's high arm relaxed and slid down to join his other arm around my waist. "What are the chances of them following us here?"

"None." Then I gave it real thought. "Virtually none. But the diagram is still there for them to figure it out if they have a mage with them. I blocked Lonnie from being able to do magic against me a long time ago, but I didn't expect him to come looking for me and snatch me himself."

"This would be the same cousin Lonnie who stole Lindis?"

I nodded, feeling his solid chest behind my head. It would be nice to rest here for a while. But there was Lonnie to deal with and there were crystals to recharge. I wiggled to free myself.

Instead of letting me go, he hauled me up as he stood. He set me on my feet and waited for me to find my balance. "Are you quite certain it is safe for me to let go? I do not wish to have my life endangered, and no woman has ever...threatened me quite like that before. If I must hold you tight for all eternity—"

I poked him in the ribs with my elbow. "Very funny. You are safe enough now, and you well know it!"

He released me, but he was not done grinning at me. "Would you have come back to save me if I had let go?"

"Absolutely not! Did you see all those swords? Nope. You'd have been skewered."

"Ah, but you did not leave me behind. You protected me, fierce little cub that you are." He chuckled. "Lindis was right. You have now saved a dragon and a wolf. I won't underestimate you again."

"Well, you wouldn't have been in any danger if you hadn't grabbed me in the first place."

He caught my shoulder with one hand. "I would not have left you there either," he said. "Nor was I likely to allow a stranger in my glen to haul you off." He flicked his eyes at Lonnie. "What shall I do with him?"

"Oh, he will be a bother, this is very sad, but true." I contemplated his prone form. "If he came to demand my help with Lindis and determines she is here, he will get himself killed attempting to kidnap her."

"And you would feel it necessary to save him, no doubt."

I didn't appreciate his humor. "Not necessarily. Do not underestimate the annoyance he can be. I promise you, a leg full of ticks has nothing on my cousin."

Derrick frowned. "What do you propose we do with him?"

"Is there any chance that you could steer him across the border, leave him with food, a message for my parents, and a map home?" I ignored Derrick's suddenly raised eyebrows. "You'll want to make sure that he doesn't get a piece of your fur or skin or he'll try a tracking spell to return here no matter how hopeless it might seem. And make sure the map only goes one way. It would probably be better if he didn't figure out you were wolf. Then again, he might think you're a dragon. Except he probably doesn't know—"

Derrick held a hand in front of my lips. I stopped babbling the worried thoughts tumbling in my head.

"How about I take care of it? You promise me no nosy questions, and I'll promise no harm will come to him—" He stopped because I was shaking my head. "Why not?"

"I will not hold you to 'no harm.' No one is that good. He'll likely spear himself on a stray stick and kill himself even if you turn him loose. Just get him out of here, and tell him I died. No, you can't do that. He might tell my parents." I frowned, thinking furiously. "Tell him to tell my mother I went the way of the birds, and all will be well. She'll know I'm okay and not worry."

Derrick had ceased listening and walked away. He flipped cousin Lonnie over his shoulder like a sack of grain and strode into the trees.

Ah, well.

Finding the cellar and five eggs took me a good fifteen minutes. Derrick hadn't returned so I took myself back into the stone house. There was one big problem awaiting me inside. My orange crystal was gone. I searched the ashes thoroughly before throwing on more wood to stoke the fire.

Either Derrick had retrieved it or someone else had while we were otherwise occupied extracting ourselves from Lonnie's clutches. The sun was set, which was also very bad. I needed the sun to recharge my large crystal since I had used the power in it to activate Lonnie's transportation spell.

Rays of sunshine were a mellow, but very strong energy source. The energy was well-rounded and easily transitioned into light, heat, or shocking force. It even did well when dribbled out slowly.

Without fully charged crystals, I was very vulnerable. If I wasn't so worn out, I could use my own energy to throw a quick spell, much as Lonnie often did. It was a dangerous and foolhardy way to work magic. And lately, when had I the energy to spare? Never.

The fire in the stove provided a quick, but small charge to my white crystal. Pulling heat into the stone that quickly cost me, and I was already very tired. The whole point in setting the spell and baking it in the fire was to let the fire gather and store energy without draining me.

Good thing scrambling eggs and grilling meat didn't require much tending because my dizziness was back, sitting right on top of exhaustion.

By the time the meal was ready, Derrick returned. He was whistling and quite smug until he saw the meal. "You could have made enough for two."

I rolled my eyes. "I've already eaten a chunk of meat. The rest is for you. I'd have prepared more eggs, but I couldn't find the other nests."

Slightly mollified he put down a jug. "Goat's milk. Still warm."

Swooning would be unladylike, but since I was light-headed anyway, it was a close call. I set two tin cups on the stove and placed the milk on the back of the stove where it was warm, but not hot. As soon as my cup heated, I drank some milk before even sitting down. "Mmm. Yum."

"I see that."

I licked the froth off my upper lip and grinned. "Sorry." I poured him a cup and refilled mine. "Unless you want the rest of the jug to go with your tiny serving of meat?"

He growled and accepted the cup, but didn't take his eyes off of my face. "You missed some."

"Oh." I licked my lips again and then, embarrassed, used my sleeve. "Good milk."

He focused on my lips as though we were about to attend church and I was a naughty child who forgot to wash her face. "Don't you want to know what I did with your cousin?" he finally asked.

"If you insist on telling me. But really, no, not right now." I sighed and sat. "Maybe never. If you tell me where the other chicken nests might be, I'll scramble some more eggs." If I didn't wander outside and fall asleep accidentally.

"This will do," he grunted. "I need to hunt later anyway."

I finished my eggs and briefly considered examining the text I had stolen from Lonnie, but my yawn convinced me otherwise. "I need a safe place to keep this," I told Derrick, touching the book. "I'm hoping it will have something in it to help me figure out how to unbind Lindis."

"Don't you need your crystals for that?" Derrick stood and collected the dishes. I moved to help him, but he waved me off. "You cooked."

"I need to recharge my white crystal because I used it to get us back here. And my orange went missing." It was hard not to sound accusatory.

He turned from the sink, a boyish grin on his face. He pulled the orange crystal from his pocket and held it up. Light from the glowing mage lantern sparked across its surface. The crystal was full of more than just reflection. "This one? Did you notice I was able to complete your glyph and tie it to my own word?"

I frowned. "How could you even see the glyphs? I didn't draw it in the ashes."

Now he smiled fully, obviously pleased with himself. "If you drew it in the air, you'd need something to orient the design with. If it were me, I'd use the cast iron plate on the stove as the border. I watched how you drew left to right and then sealed the circle with your word of power when you taught Lindis." He walked over to me, holding the crystal tightly in his fist. "I put the finishing mark on it just as you showed Lindis. If she can do it, there is no reason I can't. I don't know why no one has ever trained with mage magic here. Maybe because we don't need it as much as you humans." He looked at me then, almost as if he felt sorry for me. "You need this more than me."

I nodded my agreement. "Indeed. My white is nearly expended, and my orange is much smaller. Lindis has my other one. I definitely need to recharge those I have, and for that matter, I need to find more, especially if you intend to keep that one."

He seemed disappointed in my reaction. "Aren't you surprised it worked?"

"Why wouldn't it?"

"I don't know." He bounced the crystal in his hand, watching the light reflect off of it. "It makes no sense that we have no mages here in Wendal and you're overpopulated with them across the border."

"We don't have many shifters either."

He tilted his head. "There are some. Here, you need this more than I do. The word I chose is—"

By the time he said "word" my hand was raised. I slapped my palm across his mouth and hissed, "Don't!"

He wasn't the least bit intimidated by me. He grabbed my hand to forestall any possible further beating, but didn't slap it away. The word he said was mushed against my palm.

"I stored fire in there," I reprimanded him. "If you use your word of power, you'll likely free the fire and burn the place down!"

He didn't release my hand. When he licked his lips, his tongue tickled my palm. The sensation traveled all the way up my arm. "It's not a ward like the one for Lindis?" he asked, his words muffled.

I tugged my hand, but he kept it locked against his mouth.

"No, it's not a ward." I glared up at him. "That's the problem when you can't read the glyphs. You damn well better know what a spell does before you go shouting a word of power. Or tying your own word to glyphs you can't see, for that matter."

He licked his lips again, only this time it was more deliberate, a drawn out caress along my palm that was cool and hot at the same time. He kept his fingers tight on mine. As he spoke, his mouth nibbled at my hand. "How do I give you back the crystal then?"

I caught myself licking my own lips nervously. He mimicked the motion, his tongue sending flutters through my stomach.

Before I could decide whether to drop my eyes or grab the orange crystal and run, the door cracked with the weight of something heavy slamming against it. We both whirled and crouched in fight stances as it burst open.

Cousin Lonnie missed me by mere inches as he threw himself into the room. Half his head was bald and his shirt was torn into strips. It flapped wildly as if animated by chicken wings. He screamed, "Wooolf!" in a howl that would have done one proud.

Before I could so much as stand up straight, I was lifted over Derrick's shoulder. Being airborne saved me a direct hit from the wolf that came crashing in after Lonnie. The wolf smashed into Derrick's chest.

Sadly, Derrick had miscalculated. I hit the wall instead of the soft covers, bounced badly and landed on my butt. I rolled, extracting my dagger from my boot more out of habit than serious intent to kill Lonnie.

My cousin crawled towards the fire, keening with desperation.

Derrick and the wolf rolled into the stove, but the beast was the quicker to recover. A female, perhaps half the size of Derrick's wolf, she pivoted on a paw. She made a snarling grab at my cousin.

Too late I realized Lonnie had stuck his hand in the fire and snatched up a branch that was merrily burning on one end.

We shouted at the same time, his word of power a fraction ahead of my shout of his own word of cancellation. The end of the flaming stick sucked the fire from the fireplace behind Lonnie and roared into a fireball that, for one brief instant, engulfed the female wolf's head. With a yelp of pain, she fell back onto her haunches.

My cancellation halted the fireball before it rolled far, but when it broke apart it spattered in several clumps across the stone floor. I leapt over them, my dagger at Lonnie's throat before he had a chance to move. "Lonnie, you idiot! You'll roast us all!" He stared up at me, his eyes glassy. "Not one word, cousin. Not one word or I will finish you here and now."

A growl behind me warned that perhaps I had bigger problems than Lonnie, but he was almost always the largest problem in a room. It might be a relief to have something easier to contend with.

From behind me, Derrick stomped on flaming particles. "I thought you said keeping track of one dumb human would be easier than an entire den of cubs and it wasn't even worthy of your attention?"

Lonnie took a final shuddering breath and collapsed in an ignominious heap at my feet. He had completely spent himself creating a fireball with a barely burning branch and only his own energy to back it up.

Warily, I turned to find the female wolf snarling first at Derrick and then at me when I faced her. The fur at her neck was singed and standing straight up in warning. Gray and caramel rippled across her back as she bunched her muscles for a possible fight.

"Easy, friend. I'm just—" I blinked. At a sudden loss, I looked at Derrick. "Exactly what am I doing here?" I straightened from my crouch, feeling aches in a thousand places. "I don't know what I am doing here really. At any rate, I've no quarrel with you."

The wolf didn't agree. She took a snarling step in my direction before Derrick gave a warning growl of his own. "Star."

She snapped her teeth at him in frustration. Those teeth were closer to me than Derrick.

Derrick must not have been very worried because he did not step between us. Instead he said, "I thought you promised not to go wolf while he was under your watch? Weren't you going to prove you could handle problems without going wolf?"

She snapped her teeth again, but her tail lowered. Derrick was obviously dominant, and she was caught out.

I rubbed the bridge of my nose. "You aren't the first to discover that Lonnie is impossible," I told her sympathetically.

Derrick growled. He leaned over, checked the female's singed fur and then towered over Lonnie. "He's unconscious again."

"He over-extended himself."

"How did he find his way back here?" Derrick directed the question at Lonnie, but then moved his attention to the wolf. She plopped down on the floor, her head pillowed on her paws. She was subdued and a bit distraught.

"Probably a tracking spell." I frowned. "But if he was running at a good clip, I'm not sure how he managed that. He can't force a spell on me, which is why he needed to transport himself here and grab me physically earlier today. Apparently he did track me though. I need to devise a blocking spell to keep him from doing that." I gave a weak smile. "Been a bit too busy lately to have even thought of it."

Derrick leaned over and hoisted Lonnie over his shoulder. He indicated the open door with his head. The female wolf stood and trotted to the opening.

"Nice meeting you, Star. Come by sometime when you have time to chat."

The wolf halted with one paw in the air. Her wide-eyed look at Derrick clearly asked, "Is she serious?"

Derrick just growled, "Let's go."

By the time he returned, assuming he did, I was fast asleep. Whether he slept inside or out, wolf or man, I had no idea at all.

Chapter 10

Lindis woke us before noon. Well, Derrick might have already been awake, but my body was still buried under the covers determined to rest completely before walking again. I blinked sand out of my eyes while the angry dragon lady paced in the too-small cottage.

Derrick gave her the short and then the long side of Lonnie's greatest activities while I washed my face. I didn't hear all of the conversation, and it stopped rather suddenly when I darted from the bath to the kitchen to scrounge at the stove for warm milk and boiled eggs.

With my mouth still full, I brought out the book and showed it to Lindis. "I'm going to start here. But I also must recharge my crystals. And we need to change your crystal so that Lonnie can't track you. That's an easy fix; we just need to add a couple of glyphs."

Lindis and Derrick exchanged glances.

"What?" I asked.

"We dragons do not have a successful history with magic. We have perfect memories, although it took me some thinking to call to mind the history of magic. In this case, a spell itself interrupted the passing of certain details along genetic lines. Luckily, when I detected the gap, I went to my mother. She was alive when the spell was cast. It took some doing to keep our concentration, but it turns out magic has been forbidden to us since the last war with the humans."

"It is? But why?"

Lindis shrugged. "An old geas we agreed to in order to end the last great war about five hundred years ago. The human mages claimed they needed magic to defend against our greater strength and would stop hunting us to the death if we agreed not to practice magic. The geas meant instant death for any shifter who used magic, and it included a curse against crossing the Wendal border—by either party. Guess it's a good thing I didn't know that before I tried magic." She grinned.

"But you cross the border all the time!"

She nodded. "But only for the last century and a half. When the dividing veil was still working, anyone who traveled near it from either side of the border lost interest. Sometime in the last two centuries something destroyed the veil. I could have accessed the memories at any time, but I didn't know they were blocked. I had no reason to hunt through the great memories until now."

"A veil. Across your mind and the border." It was hard to fathom, but explained why Wendal was wrapped in such mystery and myth.

She nodded. "I've called the dragon memory to the forefront, but direct knowledge of spells and magic is still blocked. I had trouble with the memories too, but my mother had an easier time of it and trust me, when it became obvious something was blocking us, we were instantly intrigued.

"There should be written records amongst you humans. That is your usual method and the reason you keep all your books." She pointed to my most recent acquisition.

I certainly hadn't advanced far enough to have found any such records if they existed. "Mayhap, but if you were spelled to forget, perhaps the humans were spelled as well."

"There's no stories in my wolf memories either," Derrick said. "Although since we don't live much longer than most humans, it would be interesting to see if Grandfather remembers once I remind him."

Lindis agreed. "Yes, it would."

It would be nice to know everything my parents knew even if it took practice to extract it from a memory. Probably. "Do you know the glyphs that kept you from using magic and made you forget the history?"

"I can recite the agreement exactly since Mother told me, but I'm not certain she could reproduce the glyphs. I doubt the humans shared the exact spell, even though we allowed it to be activated."

"What is the agreement?" I asked, pacing away two steps.

"Humans would use no magic on us and we would use no magic at all. What with the barrier across all Wendal borders, there wasn't even trade between us for centuries. The deal was sealed with dragon and human blood. It is the dragon blood that makes the history less accessible to me."

My forehead wrinkled with thought. "If the spell required that humans wouldn't use mage magic on you, and the mages found a way around that clause, it would negate the geas that kept you from using magic. But how did someone get through the veil to use magic on someone from Wendal? Or did it collapse from age?"

Lindis shrugged. "We trade openly with Birk and have for the last hundred years. Nothing I know and nothing Mother knows tells how the veil came down or why."

"Do you think you should avoid using magic just in case it's dangerous to you?"

Lindis smiled, an evil, happy smile. "I didn't say that. I said that there was a geas that no longer seems to work. I had no reason to use magic before. I have reason to now."

"I wonder if magic has gotten stronger or weaker since the original spell?"

Derrick said, "We shifters are definitely the weaker for lack of knowing how to defend against it."

Lindis nodded. "For centuries the territories remained separate. We had no reason to venture there, but gradually in the last hundred and fifty years we traded our worst crystals to be charged as lanterns. We should have been paying more attention to the mages because whatever spell was tried on me worked just fine."

I agreed. "The binding spell was created just for you. If a wizard decided to bind me in any way, it would be a much simpler spell. Who had the time to study what would work on a dragon? And who from here helped obtain what they needed?"

"First things first," Lindis said. "The powers that be have scheduled my coming of age dance, thinking that if I am married off, it will solve the problem. The clan plans to take offers and consider options tomorrow night. I must be unbound from this ring by then or I'll fight to my own death to avoid being shackled by a forced oath that I will not keep."

My eyes widened. Good thing I wasn't still eating. "Unbind you in a few hours? It can't be done. Not unless the mage who did the spell shows up and offers to release you."

Lindis pointed to the book. "Is the answer not in there?"

"I have no idea yet." I sat and flipped a page. "Part of it maybe. But a very powerful mage had to figure out what dragon element to steal—hair, scales, maybe both. Then that mage had to come across the border or get someone from here to obtain a piece of you. Even with that accomplished, they had to figure out how to separate you from your dragon and then bind the dragon. I'm pretty sure nothing in this book is going to tell me what they took and how they managed to bind you to that ring."

"The auction is tomorrow night." At Derrick's raised eyebrow she nodded. "They can pretend it is a ball, but it's an auction at best and a gladiators ring at worst. If I'm not freed by tomorrow night every dragon except my own mother and father will agree that I must be married off to prevent infighting here and forestall my kidnapping to other kingdoms." Smoke billowed from her ears and nostrils. "I will not submit!"

I waved a hand at the smoke, batting away the emotion. "Is there no one you could choose to marry to solve the problem?"

I feared my hair would start afire just from the glare she gave me. "It's likely I will be turned over to whichever clan kills best. The winner of me would be a proven strength. Anyone who kidnapped me would then contend not only with dragons, but with whichever clan fights best to win my hand. That just means I end up with the most violent of the lot or whoever schemed and made the best deals these past weeks. Would you believe that I'd rather marry your cousin Lonnie than be forced to live under duress?"

Now I did choke, even though I wasn't eating. "No, no, I would not believe that. Trust me, being married to an inept wizard is not the answer to your problems. He'd kill you within a week based on some rumor that dragon's blood could make him fly. Or if you were really lucky you could convince him he could fly, and you could dump him over the cliff."

Derrick stood. "Maybe Zoe can convince the gladiators you are safe left alone to protect yourself. But she'll need proper attire. She's too small for your clothes. My sister's might fit." His long stride took him to the door before I realized he was leaving.

I called after him even though the door had shut behind him. "I don't think it's a good idea for me to convince anyone of anything. Especially dragons."

Lindis stared at the closed door, her eyes narrowing thoughtfully. "Do you know that had this happened a year ago, I think Derrick may have tried for my hand?"

"What makes you certain he won't try for you now?"

"He's older and smarter. He has no desire to be mated with the number one problem in Wendal. Any clan who marries me promises to fight for me, and with all the humans vying to kidnap me, right now marrying me is a promise to go to war over me."

"I can see where that might make your dowry a tad less desirable."

"His clan wants a closer alliance with dragons, but they aren't going to fight other dragons to get one. Until I was kidnapped, everyone was waiting for me to make a choice. Now that one is about to be forced on me, it becomes entirely political. At least two of the dragons will try for me even though they'd not have stood a chance before and they know it."

"You don't like any of the dragons?"

She sighed and smoke billowed again. "Remember when I said it was a rare thing for an unattached dragon to reach mating age? We live for centuries. The closest single dragons to my age are," she paused. "Let's see. Olam and Betr, who are only three hundred years older. Tawn lost his mate, so he counts. He has several grandchildren, but none will be mated this century." Desperation stopped her. She reached over and grabbed my tunic. "You must get rid of this curse!"

I struggled free of her grasp but only managed to escape because she allowed it. "Let's fix the crystal to keep Lonnie from tracking you. One suitor at a time." I withdrew my crystal to give her time to compose herself.

She slumped against the back of her chair, but her fingers drummed against the tabletop. "You do know what it means when a wolf introduces you to any of his pack members?"

It had been a mystery to me why I hadn't met any of Derrick's pack except Star, and that had not exactly been a planned introduction. Of course, most kidnapped victims weren't casually invited to family dinners. Given the hunting techniques and other clan business that likely occurred in Derrick's family, there could be a lot of reasons to keep me isolated. I met Lindis' gaze with a shrug.

She interpreted my silence correctly. "You have no idea at all." Her mouth opened, no doubt to provide me with a much-needed education, when the door opened.

Derrick led the way. Star, at least I assumed it was Star from her beautiful caramel and gray hair, pushed Lonnie in front of her. He was bound, hand, mouth and eyes. Behind Star, a taller, older and more graceful version of her followed. The silver in her hair was too rich to be from old age. The color was merely a highlight of the golds, browns and occasional streak of black.

"Lindis," the woman said in greeting before turning to me. "You must be Zoe. I'm Anne."

Like a deer, I remained quite frozen in the face of being surrounded by unknown entities. Having Lonnie thrust near me again didn't help either.

"She's much friendlier and more talkative if you threaten her, Mother."

When Derrick's mother smiled, her eyes lit up with a yellow glow. "Well, we'll see if we can't have a friendly argument while we discuss what to wear."

The wolves had their own agenda where clothing was concerned. It didn't take me long to voice admiration for the designs, especially since sewing wasn't my forte. The wolves were as talented as my own mother; taking into account beauty, design and practicality. For the wolves this meant that two quick pulls on hidden leather ties caused the dress they showed me to separate into pieces.

A wolf could easily escape her clothing without undue damage or tangling in the outfit. Any human hand could re-lace the leather through the cleverly reinforced holes stitched to accept the pressure of the ties.

I had to insist that we cut the dress in half so that the skirt could be disposed of with a separate pull of ties while the top remained. "There must be pants underneath too." I hadn't worn a dress without pants since I was six. Mother knew as well as I did that a little girl had many reasons to run—and skirts were a detriment to escaping or fighting to protect oneself.

I demonstrated how we had designed my skirts back home, by separating a few stitches in the side seam of the skirt. "The most important thing is a hidden slit through the skirt so that I can reach my dagger where I strap it to my thigh." I felt through to the petticoats. "We'll need to sew a pocket in these. And I must warn you, if you lend this to me, the dress might not come back in one piece. I've a bad habit of pulling my dagger too fast and cutting the material. There's plenty of skirt here to make the slit large and hidden, but I can't promise you it will survive."

Derrick's mother raised an eyebrow in his direction. He smiled.

Star exclaimed, "That is a great idea! The design would still work for me too when I need to change."

Derrick's smile became a frown. "Except you're working on not going wolf at the first opportunity."

"Add the slit to your own skirts too," I suggested. "If everyone expects you to go wolf or use your claws, learn to throw a dagger. That'll sit'm back a few inches." My voice was muffled by the thread I was trying to cut with my teeth.

Lindis finally looked up from the book where she was attempting to match the glyphs on her ring. "Wouldn't hurt to teach Star a trick or two with your crystals either."

"Can't," I said. "I only have one small crystal still charged, and that reminds me. I need to get the large one charging." I headed for the back door. It was very crowded in Derrick's small house. Lonnie whined at me as I stepped over his legs. "You've only yourself to blame, cousin." His presence reminded me of another problem. "I need to block you from tracking me."

I borrowed the scissors from the table where Star and her mother were still working at the outfits. Only one side of Lonnie's head still had hair, but he had more than enough for a blocking spell.

He whined again and nearly choked when he felt the scissors. "Lindis, we should add a block to yours too."

Lindis followed me outside where we could work in relative peace and quiet. If she noted my shaking hands, she didn't comment on it. Being around three wolves and a dragon was a bit trying for me. There was angst and signals that I only partially understood. My instincts kept reaching out to understand better even though I tried to tamp down on the inclination.

Derrick joined us and listened to me explain more about spells. Lindis put her hand over the yellow crystal that hung from a gold chain around her neck. When her hand came free, the crystal came with it.

"Dragons have no problem speaking to stones," she said.

Even though she had somehow threaded the crystal on and off the long gold chain, the spell and energy had remained intact. "Whatever that geas was, it didn't shut down all magic," I muttered.

"Working gems is almost as much dragon as changing from dragon to human."

"Or from wolf to human," Derrick agreed.

"Like I said. Not all the magic stopped working." I drew the symbols for recharging the crystal in the dirt. "You'll feel the power leak out of the crystal if anyone tries to track you. When the spell blocks the tracking, it's going to use up the energy. You'll want to recharge the crystal right away. Use the sun, heat, cold." I drew a connecting line to finish a particular glyph. "This symbol draws the energy into the crystal and this one stores it. If the spell isn't activated, the crystal will stay charged for a long time."

I then added a symbol to my tiny blue crystal to set a ward on myself that would keep Lonnie from tracking me.

After I finished, Lindis thanked me and gave me a last obscure warning look before retreating inside.

Derrick crouched down and offered me the orange on the palm of his hand. "I unset it like you taught Lindis to lower her wards. Does that work with this?"

"Yes."

"So you can use it now?"

I reached for it slowly, not sure if he would grab it away. He let me pluck it from his palm. "I haven't ever used one that was set and then unset by someone else. Your words are still valid on this one even though you released it. The more you use a particular word of power, the stronger it becomes especially if you tie it to the same crystal again." The stone was warm not only from his touch, but also because it retained heat from the fire. "Teach me your words. And tell me the shape of the line you used to finish the glyph. It might be good if we can both use it. If something happens to me—"

Derrick closed my fingers around the stone. "I merely followed the circle of the cast iron on the stove."

I nodded. "And the word?"

"I used the word you uttered when you threw me halfway across Lindis' room the day we met in the dragon's lair."

I had barely spoken the word in a whisper. With wolf's ears, I'd have to be more careful. "I see. Then it will be easy for me to use." I set it in the dirt and redrew the glyphs around it. As he had guessed, I worked in a circle. I could have drawn the glyphs in the air because I could see my own glyphs as motes of dancing light, but it seemed important that Derrick see the drawing too. When I said the word of power, the link snapped into place as always, but this time, energy raced up my arms like lightning carried on a breeze. The hair on Derrick's arms lifted and an errant wind blew his shoulder-length hair away from his face. It felt as though the magic raced from Derrick to me and then back again, settling across us both.

He must have felt it too because he smiled down at me with predator eyes that invited me to run. There was a promise that he would catch me, but instead of cold chills, his threat sent a different kind of electricity down my spine.

Chapter 11

Derrick's mom and Star sewed. Both of them were very fast, probably because they spent a good deal of time repairing torn wolf clothing despite the clever designs.

Derrick supplied an entire deer for dinner. I unwrapped Lonnie's eyes and after recalling the silencing spell that he had used on Lindis, I looked it up in the book. The actual spell was to cease three senses, causing a person to be temporarily deaf, blind and mute. He had either simplified the spell when he transported Lindis or had missed the proper glyphs for the deaf and blind parts.

I tied the spell to his person rather than enclosing him in a pentagram. Instead of a word of power, I used a gesture to set the spell. No one, not even the finest ears in the house, needed to learn another of my words of power.

As soon as Lonnie's gag was removed, he began making demands, albeit silent ones. I handed him a cup of water and told him to stop his silent curses.

It was back to the book for Lindis and myself, but glyphs were not easy to learn and for a lot of reasons, the instructions were obscure.

After finding a spell to enhance my dagger and applying it, Lindis shouted at me in frustration. "Parlor tricks! These are barely useful in hand-to-hand combat! We must unbind me!"

Fire licked the corners of her mouth. I tugged the tie off my braid nervously. "I'm telling you it would take an entire school of mages to figure out—" My mouth stopped as though silenced by the spell that held Lonnie's voice. My brain raced away, thinking of Gorgon where the best students were nowhere to be found and tutors could barely teach a spell. Where had those with talent gone? Had they been busy with other demands?

"What?" Lindis demanded.

"Your school burned," Derrick said. "No help there."

Calling on my schoolmates for help was not the direction of my thoughts. I was more worried about the possibility that students at Gorgon with talent had been funneled off to research dragon bindings or related spells. Those who excelled in class were interrogated heavily.

Some of them had been put into different classes, but we were all shuffled along to different classrooms so often, it was hard to keep track of where anyone went.

What if those with talent had been segregated to research binding spells? Or read up on the history of Wendal and figure out how to separate a dragon from her human counterpart? With an army of students, a lot could be learned and tested. The students wouldn't even have to know the end result or why they were studying certain aspects of spells.

I swallowed heavily. "Yeah. No help there." It did not seem like a good idea to share my sudden suspicions. If someone at Gorgon Uni were guilty, I didn't want to look guilty by association.

Besides, being surrounded by an untalented teacher or two wasn't proof that those with high magic potential had been busy elsewhere.

I flipped pages without seeing the text. It was a little coincidental that a prince happened to be right there at Gorgon ready to be kidnapped when Lindis was spelled. Who had known he was there and decided to use him to wedge an alliance with Anton? Or had someone convinced him to go there because they knew the ring was ready to hold Lindis captive?

The room was decidedly quiet. I looked up to find everyone staring at me. It was time to face facts. I couldn't undo something as complicated as a binding spell in an afternoon, even if we found a few symbols in common with the ring. If there was one thing I had learned about court politics, it was how to keep up appearances. "We're going to have to come up with a plan," I said. "I can study this book all day, but there simply isn't time to learn how to unbind you. What we need is something that makes people believe you are safe and in control of your dragon. Our best bet is to buy some time before they throw you into the marriage pen."

"It would be better to unbind me," Lindis snarled.

"Sometimes all you have is illusion, and thanks to Lonnie's illusionary dragon spells, I know how to create more than one illusion." I stood. "We'll need an ornate ring that resembles the one that binds you." Ordinarily that might not be easy to come by, but in this case, the solution had dropped in on us, uninvited. And the good news was that Lonnie had never bothered to carve more than a petty spell or two into the many baubles he wore on his fingers.

I marched over to my cousin and picked across the selection of gaudy, but nearly worthless rings on his hand. He didn't protest other than to roll his eyes. "We can duplicate enough of the glyphs on the binding ring to fool casual observers." I plucked the ring that I judged to have the most gold in the band. Handing it to Lindis, I urged, "Try it on. We're going to need a large gem to set in it, although I can use illusion to make just about any stone resemble the sapphire in yours."

Lindis smiled. "Gems are never a problem for a dragon. Neither is the shape."

"That's good. Illusion is much easier if I'm only shifting reality, not having to try and paint over it with something entirely different." I inspected the real ring against Lonnie's ring. "We'll need to carve a couple of lines here and here."

Lindis snapped forth a talon. "This gold has some impurities mixed in, but it's soft enough that it shouldn't be a problem. You want exact copies of the glyphs?"

I shook my head vehemently. "No. I'll show you which lines to leave off. We don't need to call trouble we don't fully understand."

"I'll go obtain a sapphire."

"While you're doing that, I'll double check the glyphs for the illusion." I knew them by heart, but I'd never done one this important. It wouldn't hurt to have the illusion spelled on the ring twice. After all, a sapphire was capable of holding considerably more energy than my crystals. If the first spell were somehow destroyed, maybe the second one would hold.

I sat back down and began organizing the glyphs I wanted to use. Too bad there wasn't time to invent one for myself. I could use a spell that made me look confident and knowledgeable, because the truth was, we were headed into the dance with a plan that made about as much sense as the ones Lonnie came up with.

Even if the magic worked, I had a bad feeling the flaws in the idea would show through.

Chapter 12

The climb into the dragon's lair was not nearly as strenuous as Derrick had described, but he assured me that the tunnels had been opened and smoothed for the dance because everyone was pretending to be friends and honored guests, at least for the moment.

"I still think she should pretend to pick someone," I grumbled.

Derrick was not breathing hard, but then he had slowed his normal pace to allow me to keep up. He was a sight to behold, dressed in a winter-white wool tunic and kidskin pants that allowed him a great range of movement. The perfectly tailored clothing accentuated his muscular frame. His mother was as clever with a needle as my own, and she had a very attractive son to display her work.

My fancy dress had been altered to remove two cotton petticoats at the waist. This provided a better fit for my pants underneath. Each layer had been combined at the side seam to form a slit, making my dagger easily accessible. Derrick's mother had changed out the panels on the top of the dress to a dark blue to reflect my eyes. More importantly, it made the small blue crystal sewn at the bottom of the panel a nearly invisible decoration.

The orange crystal was inset along the back of the high neckline, obscured by my hair, which she insisted I leave down. How was I supposed to fight with my hair flying all over the place?

Her idea that this was Lindis' battle was all well and good, but failed to reassure.

The room where the auction, or rather dance, was to be held was not a sight for mere mortals. It wasn't just the beauty of the stalactites across the ceiling, it was the sparkle of embedded gems and crystals that called to magic as surely as did the precise round formation of the room itself. The cavern had to have been designed with glyphs in mind even if the dragons had managed to forget magic for a while.

Fireplaces at either end were perfect markers; their shape not unlike a glyph. Swords were set high along the walls, some crossed, some angled—all a part of a mysterious pattern that was unreadable to my untrained eyes, but could easily provide the start and finish to important spells. The settings were too intricate to be mere decoration. Mayhap the dragons would have to work to remember the magic, but this room was meant to house it.

The floor was a forestland of stalagmites. While some of the formations were a dancing maze of color, strategically selected stalagmites had flattened tops, turning them into tables and chairs. Fountains flowed across the room, creating a open, outdoor atmosphere. Crystalline lanterns provided shadows and light, but my eye was drawn again and again to the crystals embedded in the walls. None were the shabby quality of my own, which were a good deal better than many. Almost all crystals in Birk were of lamp quality; that is to say scarred by granite or other stone, cracked or distorted such that they were useless for storing energy for spells. Any that were good enough were prohibitively expensive, which was why I only owned a barely serviceable large and three very small ones. All of mine had been cut or chipped off larger pieces that appeared nearly worthless at first glance.

"Look at them all," I exclaimed. "Do you know how impossible it is to get such high quality crystals—"

Derrick snaked his arm around my waist, pulling me against his chest so quickly, it surprised me silent. We were dancing across the open ballroom before I grasped what was happening.

"It's probably better you not tell everyone what you consider a valuable commodity." His voice was barely audible, a whisper of sweet nothings against my ear.

"Few people use them like I do," I muttered back. Of course, that was because there weren't many spares lying around to use. "Lots of wizards use metal. Or a wooden staff. Or, if they are nobles, they use real gems."

Derrick pressed my head onto his chest and spun me faster.

"Derrick, you're going to smother me!"

"Only if you don't cease talking," he murmured. "My little cub," he added a bit louder.

He released my head, but ducked his own to nuzzle my neck. The room carried hints of fires and food, but in one deep breath, the scent was all Derrick, a spicy cinnamon mixed with deep forest. In another time and place...I stepped on his foot. Twice, rather hard. Electric shivers or not, I didn't like to be part of such a public display. "Must you make a spectacle of us?"

He spun us around again, laughter lighting his face. "If you continue to provide me an excuse, I shall." With great skill, he stepped back, directed me under his arm and back to him again. Good thing mother had trained Lonnie to dance, and I had learned as a byproduct. At last, a reason to be grateful to cousin Lonnie.

The thought caused an uncomfortable prickling between my shoulder blades. Star and her mother were not about to be left out of the dance after sewing my dress all afternoon. That left Lonnie closeted with a pack member who was completely inexperienced with wizards. Lonnie remained silent because of the spell on him, but he was still Lonnie. "You really should have shipped him across the border with a one-way map and—"

Derrick reeled me in again, pulling me so close my breasts were smashed flat against him. "You're such a tease," he whispered.

If I could have spared the energy in the crystal, I'd have blasted him across the room. Well, at the very least singed his fingers a bit. "Derrick!"

"That might have been borderline," he admitted, tilting my head back with his thumb along my jaw. He dipped me slightly, his fingers splayed against my neck in a warm caress against my skin.

I ceased babbling because for half a second, we were frozen in time with him staring into my eyes as if I were the only woman in the room. He leaned closer as if he would kiss me. My breath caught.

The music required that he move and he did. He kept me close, spun me around and began talking. He provided details about those around us, randomly, as if he weren't paying attention to his own words.

It took me more than one pass to focus. Derrick danced so expertly, most people were little more than a swirl of colors. There was some sense of who was what by their attire. Most of the female dragons wore gowns of sheer silk with huge hoops that mimicked the shape of a dragon. The men didn't hesitate to allow wisps of smoke to float about their heads as though they were indulging in cigars rather than partaking in male dragon showmanship.

Derrick pointed out his father, a lithe man as tall as he, but broader. Derrick seemed only a bit older than me. He couldn't be much more than twenty. His shoulders might well equal his father's in a couple more years. Fleetingly, I wondered what it would be like to partner permanently with someone who had the assurance and confidence of a noble without the strings.

Next we swirled by a couple that Derrick identified as "Bear clan." It was all rather too much to take in, as were the quick political notes that he barely whispered about hawks, foxes and gryphons.

"Gryphons?" I echoed, trying but failing to see who he was talking about.

"A rare event, indeed, although the dwarves showing up is even more puzzling."

"Everyone is interested in aligning with a dragon," I guessed.

"Not the dwarves. They are a solitary lot. The gryphons often use their abandoned tunnels as lairs, and lately the dwarves appear to be friendlier with them, as opposed to just tolerant. As for the gryphons, they have always expressed interest in a closer alliance with the dragons. Their territory is similar to that of the dragon, as is their lifespan." He shrugged. "We have little quarrel with the dwarves or the gryphons at the moment, but in times like these, alliances and agreements become suspect."

Because someone had kidnapped a dragon and wanted to use her against Wendal. If Lindis were aligned with the mages in any kingdom, things could change here and quickly. They were already changing and a mage in control of a dragon was a powerful threat indeed.

Still straining to see the gryphon, I caught only a glimpse of long green robes before Derrick turned us again. Finally back around, I spotted him, forest colors for dress and the white hair of a learned...mage.

My feet stopped moving entirely and had Derrick not picked me up, he would have tripped over my unmoving form.

"Zoe?"

I stared. My head swiveled on its own when Derrick twirled me away from my target. I couldn't find my feet. They were no longer part of my body. If only the roaring in my ears would subside. I clutched Derrick's shoulders and finally tore my gaze away. The craggy features of the mage were burned into my vision. I knew him, there was no doubt.

Barely able to speak, I asked, "Have you noticed how round the room is? And the dance floor, too, for that matter." How easy it would be to encase the entire room in a spell circle. The notes of music drifted through the air one at a time as slow as my thoughts.

"Zoe? You're paler than the sun." He shook me lightly and backed me off the dance floor to the fire.

"Derrick—"

The song ended and changed to a soft background. It was nearly time for Lindis to make her entrance. She controlled the illusion, but for how long? Derrick's hand on the small of my back guided me towards one of several exits. Each arched stone opening had a crystalline light on either side, illuminating people as they came and went. Lindis would arrive on the stage according to custom.

It did not surprise me to see her enter from a side door even as we walked towards a different opening. She posed in the lights for just long enough to be noticed. Her eyes swept the room and when hers caught mine, she grinned. Those nearest her gasped and sudden chatter caught like wildfire.

Lindis was decked out full dragon style, layers of purple, black and iridescent white silk fashioned to resemble dragon scales. The skirt was wide enough to easily accommodate her dragon body when she changed, supported from behind by a wide hoop. Where my stride didn't do my dress justice, she moved as though she were gliding in for a perfect landing.

Her black hair shimmered and reflected light as if it were as hard as a dragon scale. With her natural coloring, she would never be forced to rely on face paints to enhance her appearance.

"You could do worse than have a mate such as her." I wasn't really talking to Derrick, but it was true. She was beautiful. Deadly. Powerful. And that was just the woman.

Derrick moved his arm further around my waist. "Or I can do better."

My laugh was brittle from the worry sweating through my pores. The pressure to tell him was unbearable even though telling him would make me instantly suspect and untrustworthy by association. I stood on tiptoe to be as near his ear as possible. He secured my balance with both hands at my waist.

"The gryphon you pointed out." I paused and took another deep breath. "The gryphon is the mage-master at Gorgon." When he did not react, I added, "Hewitt's father, remember? He was in charge of Gorgon and had access to an unimaginable array of mage talents. He also apparently has access to Wendal. And Lindis. He must be the one who set the binding spell on the ring."

Derrick's hands dropped from me as though scorched. "The father of your cub?"

"What?" I expected his reaction to be harsh. He would have no choice but to brand me guilty. I had been at Gorgon training for an entire year. I had left there with Hewitt and showed up at an ill-fated, coerced wedding ceremony. Gorgon was the perfect place to gather wizardly strength, and I had come from there. Even to myself I looked guilty.

Derrick's eyes blazed wolf yellow.

There was no time to defend myself. I had promised Lindis I would be a supporting actress in her play. But how could I help if Derrick announced me as the traitor?

The muttering around us grew in volume as Lindis announced, "I will take no mate. By my right, I will choose when I am ready and not before. The curse which bound me has been removed." She had chosen to make her stand in the middle of the dance floor rather than take the stage. Just as we had practiced, she ripped the ring from her finger and threw it to me.

I twisted my body around to catch it.

It was then that I expected Derrick to shove me aside and accuse me, but he was an unmoving stone wall. The ring twirled through the air, catching the lights. Lindis, her finger appearing naked, began her change.

I caught the ring and covered it with my fist. Noise exploded across the room. Lindis went full dragon, challenging anyone to defy her wishes. Her dress expanded and it was hard to tell what was silk and what was dragon. A very nice distraction and camouflage for any attacking swords.

My eyes tracked around the room to Master Alcen. The gryphon, the mage from the School of Gorgon, had sidled closer to Lindis.

"Does he claim you?" Derrick demanded in a dangerous growl.

"What?" Derrick was supposed to be watching for the naysayers or those who might threaten Lindis. I expected him to either gut me as the enemy or at the least, restrain me. How to convince him that it was not me he needed to be worried about?

His arm on mine, he shook me hard enough to rattle my teeth. "Why does the gryphon not claim you if you bore him a child?"

My attention finally locked on Derrick. A continuous low growl rumbled from his chest. Even as I watched, his hair lengthened and his snarling face changed even more. "Derrick! What are you talking about?" He was obviously still working through my involvement, but was on the wrong track. "The gryphon is married to another, and besides that, Hewitt is not mine. Alcen is a master mage! If anyone could spell the ring, it is he. If he did not do it, he had the entire resources of Gorgon at his disposal!"

Derrick's eyes glowed the surreal of the wolf. I wasn't even certain he heard me.

In one quick leap, the gryphon took the stage where Lindis should have been. He spoke loudly enough for all to hear. "It would seem some are up to your challenge, little dragon. Maybe you will fight them all to the death?"

It was hard to ignore the fact that the gentleman standing next to me had just turned into a black panther. Derrick never took his eyes off me, but from one instant to the next he was man and then wolf.

This was not in the script.

"And can you change back at will, Lindis?" The way the gryphon said her name was wrong. He hissed it, sounding a lot like Lindis did when she set her own spells. Something of her was in the ring. Oh, this was bad indeed. He had guessed the illusion we tried or was testing it.

"Lindis, my pet," he crooned.

Lindis raised a talon, the one with the invisible ring. The gesture was a hesitant, longing one; that of a lover reaching for her beloved.

The mage-master had created the ring, and he knew how to call it to him.

"Lindis!" I cried desperately.

But Lindis' eyes focused on the gryphon with an all-encompassing intensity.

I ripped the orange crystal from the back of my neck and drew the glyphs that would mute the mage. Derrick was supposed to guard me if I had to spell, but he was no longer at my side. Too bad. I had to stop the mage-gryphon from calling Lindis!

Even as I spelled, Lindis took a halting step towards the stage where Master Alcen waited. Lindis' parents, in full dragon form, flanked her, waiting for some indication of what she wanted. Lindis' father had been in basic black with silver embroidered scales across his attire. Changed, he looked much the same except that his silver tipped scales were honed to deadly points. Lindis' mother flashed maroon scales and talons long enough to be used as a spit over a fire.

I surged my way through the crowd, struggling to reach the stage. The bodies were a solid wall of creatures. Large and small, all with the deadly weapons of their shifted forms, they milled in the air, on the ground, on the tables and probably swam in the pools.

"Perhaps you wish to make a choice after all, my sweet dragon?" Master Alcen was dangerous enough as a mage, but even as I watched, his body rippled. The body of a lion with magnificent wings was now center stage. Only his face remained that of a man. In full fighting form, his head would be that of an eagle.

A dwarf suddenly appeared behind him, taking up a defensive position at his back.

"Lindis!" I had to redo the glyphs. There was no way I could cast my mute spell on a gryphon. He would claw me into the next life with one swipe even if I managed to reach the stage.

In confusion, Lindis hunted me in the crowd. Her eyes brimmed with pain, and her talons drew blood again as she clutched the ring with hatred and need.

"Change back, my dear. There is no need for your dragon here," Master Alcen crooned.

Lindis obeyed. Being human left her at an extreme disadvantage against every beast in the room.

I hurriedly reset the stone with the other glyph from the spell I had just learned. It might not work. I still didn't understand any of the magic in the ring, and my magic was simple by comparison.

Before I could work my way to Lindis, a meaty fist grabbed my hair and the back of my dress, yanking me off my feet.

"Give it to me!" The snarl was deep, but fully human. A star-shaped scar crested the forehead of the man who shook me like a bag of stale bread. My mouth dropped open. *Camden, the Anton warrior from the church!* And the bastard had me in a death grip. If he recognized me, it was all mixed in with the anger he shouted in my face. The same colors he wore at the church graced his frame now: the green and gold of Anton. The only difference was that this time I could smell the garlic on his breath and see the new scar from Brittany's well-placed shot.

He shouted, "The dragon will be mine!"

His claim warranted the gryphon's attention. "I think not."

The warrior turned his green-eyed gaze to him and snarled, "Oh, I think so. She had her chance at prince blood. If she can accept you, then she can accept me."

The gryphon laughed, a sound that was more lion than human. "I believe our agreement is over."

"Lindis," I gasped out, hoping to gain her attention long enough to throw the crystal to her.

With the gryphon distracted, rage burned across Lindis' features and smoke poured from her ears. She may have recognized my captor as the Anton warrior from the church or not. Either way, she ignored me and reached behind the now ill fitting dress to pull her sword. With a single swipe, she dared anyone to stop her.

The warrior who restrained me sensed victory as the gryphon's hold on Lindis eased.

I tossed the fake ring he wanted so badly far into the crowd.

Without hesitation, he flung me backwards and went after it.

A hard wolf body stopped me from spiraling into the fire, but it was

Star rather than Derrick. She gave me a wolfish grin and pushed me back into the crowd. With lupine grace, she created a path through the bodies, winding and pushing so that I could follow.

The gryphon called softly, "Lindis, my pet."

She halted, her sword arm jerking back. She pivoted towards the mage, her eyes glassing over even as she fought to bring her arm under her own control.

"Lindis!" I dove through legs; man and furred ones alike.

Her free hand trembled, but reached for me. My hand clasped hers and with my heart and soul, I mouthed the word. Her fingers curled around the crystal. The power drained from it, surrounding her ears with an invisible cage. Fear spread across her features as all sound ceased. With a gasp, she grabbed for her head. Forgetting her sword, she nearly sliced her own face.

Being smacked with one's own sword apparently helps engage the brain.

The gryphon called to her again, but she could not hear. There was no chance she would understand his words, never mind obey them if she couldn't hear them.

The spell had worked! She was as deaf as Lonnie.

Strong arms dragged me backwards. Derrick whispered, "Be still." He kept me close against his chest as he pushed through the crowds. His tunic flapped loose, but he had managed to secure his pants.

Without even bothering to sheath her sword, Lindis changed back to dragon. She reached for the gryphon, and this time, it in no way resembled a caress. He met her change by completing his own.

I wasn't certain what damage he could do as a gryphon or a wizard, but Lindis was obviously going for "dead wizard as soon as possible."

She threw a fireball that the gryphon deflected with magic.

In the battle that was the dance floor, the Anton warrior roared victory. He held the ring I had thrown high above the crowd.

Lindis was too busy stalking her prey to notice and couldn't hear him anyway.

That didn't deter him. "By the shores of Anton, by my own name, I command you to return to your ring!"

"Uh-oh." He must have had a hand in spelling the ring. His final shout of "Camden" rang across the hall.

I prayed, but it was to no avail. The owner of the ring appeared anyway.

Cousin Lonnie was not part bird, and in fact could not fly at all. He ricocheted off a stalactite on his way down, clipped the wing of a flapping dragon, and bounced off a lion before rolling to the feet of the now speechless mage-warrior from Anton.

Chapter 13

As Derrick dragged me backwards, he whispered sweet nothings in my ear, or they may as well have been because I couldn't hear a thing with the roar of noise that was Camden on the warpath. The rush to Lindis was on, but she screamed defiance as she attacked the gryphon. Her parents flanked her, holding back any that might interfere.

Derrick's strong arms kept me close, my feet off the ground, as he worked his way out of the throng of bodies. He finally set me down next to one of the exits. Since everyone else was busy fighting a battle or watching one, no one paid any attention to us, not even cousin Lonnie who was completely prone and defenseless after his fall.

"The warrior who calls himself Camden walked the perimeter of the room before he grabbed you. I didn't see him start, but he ended here." Derrick indicated the doorway. "What did he do?"

Detecting spell glyphs unless they were mine or were drawn in a physical medium such as ashes was impossible. Even though I could see the path of the glyphs I drew myself, the magic was more a beam of mixed lights and floating motes. Reading my own after the fact was possible, but markers or existing shapes still helped me create the right shapes and keep everything in a known area.

"Oh no." The room was the perfect shape. One word or gesture and the Anton warrior could trap everyone inside the circle. He might have used the floor or the wall as his guide, but without knowing where or how to break the lines, it was hopeless. And without being able to see the glyphs, I might only change the spell, but not prevent it. If he wanted to turn us all into pigeon-toed goats, it would be impossible to stop him.

I shook my head. "He helped set the ring, which means he's a lot more powerful than I am."

Even as we talked, Camden marched towards the stage, sword out and doing damage to anyone in his way. Cousin Lonnie remained ignored, but no worse for the wear, on the floor. The walls around me showed no sign of glyphs. "I don't know how to prevent the spell if he triggers it!"

Derrick said, "He paused as though talking as he walked. I wouldn't have noticed except you told me to watch for such. His hands were in constant motion as he moved around the room."

Derrick had paid attention to our plan, watching people as promised. He didn't look angry anymore, but then, he expected me to pull a miracle out of my crystals. "Derrick, I can't discern what he did. I only undo Lonnie's spells because he's about as talented as a four year old drawing everything plain as day in the sand..." My voice trailed off as I thought of a real four year old. "Hewitt."

Derrick glanced through the archway. "The cub? Where?" A nearby fight pushed a combatant into the wall next to me. Before I could so much as squeak a warning, the two struggling bodies knocked me over.

Derrick grabbed one of them and threw him backwards. He then slammed his fist into the still human body of a man whose face had changed into that of a snapping badger. Before the badger hit the ground, Derrick flung him back into the crowd as well.

A quick assessment of the stage area told me we were running out of time. Lindis was half the size of the gryphon. She prevented him from weaving glyphs or throwing spells by keeping up a constant attack. Her parents kept others at bay, but the gryphon was physically more powerful than her, if not as desperate.

Camden was near the stage now, close enough to engage Lindis' parents—or close enough to cast the spell he had set.

Derrick had shown me the basic path of the glyphs. Hewitt had shown me how to use a stick across a circle to break it. But I couldn't float a stick in the middle of the doorway. "Watch my back," I yelled above the din. "I need to make a door that I can swing open."

The crystal lights on either side of the arch didn't extend far from the wall, but they and the floor in front of the door could serve as my outline. All I needed was something solid to move if the circle locked...would one of the swords on the wall work?

Too obvious. And big. If someone kicked it out of the way before the rest of the circle was locked, it would dissolve my "door."

Another crystal? Not long enough.

I needed a thick door, as wide as possible. It had to be more reliable than the stick Hewitt had used. When Camden snapped the circle closed, the door had to be large enough to cover the glyph area, but mobile. If it worked right, the door would open and unlock the circle. Hopefully.

The only problem was that I wasn't Hewitt and had no foresight into where the last lines of the glyph would be.

Another worried glance found Camden on the stage. Whatever he was going to do wouldn't wait much longer. I pulled my dagger and laid it from the opening straight into the room. My door was going to have to be made of glyphs tied to the dagger and my crystals. The dagger would serve as the physical, movable anchor. The largest crystal would tie the magic together. I didn't want my puny power snuffed out under Camden's greater strength.

My dagger was nothing more than a discarded weapon, lost in the mess of discarded clothing, tufts of fur, food and blood...The dagger was small, more like a doorknob. Hewitt had turned the entire stick, erasing a portion large enough to step through.

"Derrick! The lacing from your trousers—I need a large piece of the leather tie."

Despite the danger around us, he spared the time to raise a suggestive eyebrow. "I can take them off entirely if need be."

"Just the binding from one side, but hurry. Here," I flipped my dagger around. "Cut off a good length of the leather strip. The longer it is, the more I can account for where his spell might be."

Derrick accepted my dagger, but held my eyes while he sliced the leather tie that was the outside seam. The leather was made to give, to loose the wolf with the least amount of hampering.

I snatched the bottom length as he unraveled the other end.

I began the spell, using the thin leather strip to form a rectangle base across the floor, straight across the exit.

Would it be enough? It certainly covered more area than the dagger.

My white crystal responded readily to the power in the two lanterns across the arch. It was a simple matter of feeding the magic into the rectangle on the floor all the way up to the lanterns. Even though parts of the design had no physical anchor, it formed a doorway-like magical formation. Not my best spell, maybe, but it might work. If magic snapped across it, the rectangular shape would be mine to move.

"Now, we hold here." The leather could too easily be displaced by a scuffle. I stood on the opposite side of the archway from Derrick, my dagger back in my hand where it belonged and my teeth bared. It was laughable. The creatures all around me had far more lethal teeth. Without Derrick, there wouldn't have even been calm to set the spell, never mind guard it.

We didn't have long to wait.

Chapter 14

When Camden reached the stage, there should have been two large angry dragons to fight him off. Instead, he paused and slashed his own hand with the tip of his sword. He crouched in a fighting stance, very low. It took me too long to realize he was drawing the final glyph on the floor of the stage. I felt the snap of the circle, completing not only the last few feet of the doorway, but stretching to the blood glyph he drew in the apex of the room.

Because shock kept me motionless, I didn't at first realize the damage that was done. Camden raised his sword and in the blink of an eye the gryphon's head rolled across the stage. The effort of separating it from the torso drove Camden to his knees.

The fountain of blood largely missed him and sprayed Lindis and the other two dragons. Despite the bloody bath, none of the dragons moved. It didn't even look as though they were breathing.

"Derrick—" My eyes shifted, but my head did not turn. His glowing yellow eyes met mine in a panic that echoed in the protests vibrating around the room. None of the shifters were moving. Derrick's muscles bulged with his efforts. His face contorted in pain.

From the stage, Camden panted, "Time to go, my lovely." A river of sweat dripped down his brow. He barely made it to his feet. The effort of closing the circle with a spell powerful enough to freeze us in our tracks caused him to sway unsteadily. His hands were shaking almost violently, but it didn't stop him from reaching for Lindis' talon and the ring that was there, hidden only by my illusion of a dragon scale.

Darting movement on the other side of the exit near me caught my attention. I couldn't turn far enough to see who it was, but the flicker of motion was low to the ground and fast. "Star?" Could she open my rectangle? My head refused to swivel enough to see if it was a tunnel rat, a wolf or my imagination. I could see most of the leather tie lying miles out of my reach. On the stage where my head had been turned, Camden searched for and located the invisible ring on Lindis' finger. He yanked it free.

"No!" My protest was lost in the cacophony of voices uselessly screaming in the wind.

Lindis, separated from the ring, gave a heart-wrenching shriek and changed back to human form. Camden caught her naked body over his shoulder.

To the side of me, a very small human hand grabbed the ends of the leather tie. The rectangle moved partway before the hands changed positions to the other side so that the rectangle stayed intact as it was slid bit by bit. The string slowly edged backward.

Between one breath and the next there was an immense snap of energy, a vibration that knocked me to my knees.

Crack!

The power broke free with an audible bang, recoiling back across the glyphs and shattering more than one crystal along the circle.

My head spun so fast my neck bobbed with pain.

Derrick raced for the stage, shoving bodies out of the way. Two angry dragons reached for Lindis, but they fell on empty air.

"Hewitt," I gasped. "What are you doing here?"

He dropped the leather tie and reached up to put his hand in mine.

"You're crazy!" I screeched at him. But what could I do? He had no protection, no friends and the room was full of weapons that included swords, claws, talons, beaks and very sharp teeth. His father's head was a bloody stump.

I grabbed him up, piggyback style, and told him to hang on. "Do not get yourself speared back there. Warn me early if a knife comes!"

Before he was fully settled, I pushed towards the stage, but it was long since too late. Camden had transported Lindis away. If he thought Lindis would be an easy mark without her dragon form, he was in for a very large and hopefully deadly surprise.

"Snap his neck, dig out his spleen and feed him to the fish," I whispered. Even assuming Lindis was giving Camden the fight of his life, she might need help. But how to find out where she had been taken and how to get her back?

* * *

It was a long night, especially carrying around a mostly sleeping Hewitt on my back. The now dead Master Alcen had obviously had some magical control over the ring, but unlike Camden, he had been clever about hiding his magic. Other than drawing Lindis to the stage by request, he had only worked magic when he stopped a flaming ball of fire aimed at his head. There were plenty of people who denied it was magic and only luck. Most of them were gryphons.

I knew better than to believe the fire had petered out on its own before reaching him.

Still, the gryphon clan clung to excuses and refused to believe there was any reason for war with the dragons. The dragons were of another mind entirely. They threw the gryphons out of the cliffs with the exception of the two highest ranking ones, who were imprisoned.

That action would, no doubt, be enough to get a nice war started soon enough.

The dragons controlled the tunnels, sealing off the climbable entryways. The openings became nothing more than a rock face. We were locked in stone that only a dragon could open. No one was leaving unless they happened to have a transport spell at the ready.

Derrick informed me that the less I said, the better, so when Lindis' father collared me and hissed, "Give me one reason I shouldn't kill you," I remained mute.

Hewitt slid off my back. Smart kid, but it made me very nervous about the outcome of this particular confrontation. Not only was the dragon much larger than me in any form, using magic in the chaos that was trying to organize itself seemed like something only Lonnie would be dumb enough to try. Thinking of Lonnie made me break out in a sweat.

"Jared, she can still assist us." Derrick reappeared by my side, almost faster than if he had used magic. "Her past help should be reason enough to leave her alive."

"She failed," the dragon roared.

Couldn't argue that.

"She isn't the one who kidnapped Lindis." Derrick's voice cut with the threat and promise of a fight.

Was he crazy? We were trapped in stone walls controlled by dragons. They could toast and roast both sides of us before we took the first step to run.

"She didn't protect her from being stolen away when it mattered most!" Jared was not mollified by Derrick's attempt at logic.

"Actually, she did." Derrick folded his arms. "Twice. How many times do you expect her to rescue Lindis before you dragons take care of your own business?"

Jared turned his wrath on Derrick. "About the time there are no human mages left to interfere in our business."

"Like the humans wanted to get rid of the dragons during the last war? That didn't work out for them. It might not work out so well for the dragons either."

Hewitt reappeared, sliding into his customary spot under one of my hands. He offered me the orange crystal that I had passed Lindis to block her hearing. She must have dropped it in the scuffle. Next, to my great surprise, Hewitt held up a shiny gold loop for my inspection. I recognized it immediately. "From Camden?" Lindis must have torn off Camden's hair clip before he transported her away.

Hewitt smiled.

"What would you do if I took your hatchling?" Jared hissed at me.

My eyes slid to Derrick. This was not good. I had just finished convincing Derrick that Hewitt was not my cub. I pushed Hewitt behind me. "Don't," I said. Unlike Derrick's steady growl, my voice shook.

A woman with maroon eyes stepped in front of Jared then. He protested, "Roelle!"

She ignored her husband and asked, "Can you find Lindis again or not?" Her eyes were not the gentle orbs of a weeping mother. They brimmed with an intense rage that included smoldering flames.

My fingers curled around the gold band. "Maybe."

"Before or after she is compromised?" Jared was not finished with me.

"You don't ask much, do you?" Derrick intervened again.

Lindis' father had him by the throat before anyone else could move. "You overstep, wolf!"

Four dragons, steam coming from their ears and throats, and two large wolves suddenly surrounded Derrick and Jared. Shouting ensued about agreements, alignments and fault.

I lifted Hewitt to my back again. Lindis' mother gave me a nod and pulled me aside. "Find her. Compromised or not. I assure you she will not care and in time no one else will either. I want her alive." Her voice hitched into a funny hiss. "Alignment." She spat. "Just alive."

"I can't do it from here."

"Of course not." She started to drag me away, but I dug my feet in. "I need Derrick and Star to come with me," I said. "And that will mean the rest of his clan unless one of them chooses to stay to hear the rest of the politics." If I left without Derrick, living until morning was a dicey prospect. Not everyone here sounded interested in retrieving Lindis; after all, a dead Lindis was a problem solved. Those same factions could easily decide to halt any helpful little mages who might try to find and return Lindis to her clan. Without Derrick to guide me, I didn't know friend from foe. Without him to protect me, I didn't stand a chance.

"You are not in a position to demand anything."

I kept my head down, but spoke the truth, one desperate woman to another. "And you're asking a lot for someone who doesn't have any idea what's involved in tracking her down."

Her talons bit into my arm and drew blood. "If you fail, I will hunt you and yours to the deepest pit."

The pain in my arm made me angry. This mess was not of my doing. "Meanwhile, you might want to sift through your veiled memories. The geas has been broken. You used magic at one time. You're going to need it again, especially if I fail." I lifted my head and met her silver glare. "Dragon blood was used in the spell that binds your daughter. After what I've seen here tonight, it had to be Lindis' own blood, and that means you have a traitor in your midst. Trust me when I tell you I'm not your biggest problem."

She shoved me against a wall. "Wait here."

The fireplace still flickered with a few flames, but in order to recharge a crystal, I needed to be closer to it. The flat-topped stalagmite chairs weren't positioned right, but the spiral column I was half behind blocked at least some prying eyes. Maybe if I pretended to warm my hands or dropped something a bit closer to the flames...

Before I could make up my mind, a giant hawk landed on a platform that jutted out from the pearlescent column. He changed as he landed, remaining clothed in golden brown and white-tipped feathers. His feet stayed clawed, but his head had a light covering of golden brown hair. Abnormally long tapered fingers looked as though they might revert to wing tips at a moment's notice.

Instead of a smooth deep voice, his was scratchy and staccato. "So. You are the little sorceress who was to help Lindis. And you disappointed."

I encouraged Hewitt to stay close, as in behind me, but he plopped down on the floor next to my feet instead. Out of the corner of one eye, I saw Star take notice of the hawk. She left her guard post next to cousin Lonnie and moved quickly through the crowd.

If the hawk's approach was newsworthy to someone in Star's clan, it was probably past time for me to lose the skirt in preparation for more fighting. Instead, with a sigh, I sat next to Hewitt on the floor. Hopefully, it would be harder to disembowel me down here. "No, I'm just the idiot who was in the wrong place at the wrong time. I'm not even a half-mage yet."

"Yet even with such a colossal failure, you have been granted the protection of the wolves. Interesting."

I shrugged. "The dragons failed at the task as well. Why should I be held to a higher standard?"

His piercing eyes widened briefly and then he chuckled. "Indeed."

When I didn't break the silence, he finally said, "I've a message for the wolves. If they wish to remain aligned, a meeting. At the noon roost tomorrow. Can you manage a message, little mage-who-is-not?"

He reminded me of the king and his advisers, implying I was somehow dysfunctional because I was a mere woman or a failed mage or both. Then again, perhaps all hawks thought it their right to taunt failures. "Who shall I say the message is from?"

Now his eyes narrowed and the claws of his feet flexed. "You're a rather insulting little human, aren't you?"

I shrugged. "You might recall that I'm not from Wendal, and we haven't been formally introduced." A plan began to form in the back of my mind. The feathers across his chest ruffled as though there were a gentle wind through the cavern. I didn't feel any such cooling relief from my less than comfortable perch on the floor.

"Shae is my name," he intoned.

I inclined my head. "Zoe of Central, Birk. My parents are merchants; Mother a seamstress and Father works metal, including some of the finest weapons in the kingdom. They are well-known in Birk." I went with the most formal introduction because of the plan lurking in my head. "Your acquaintance will be a boon."

"Of course."

Ah, the politics of social circles. His response could be affirmation of any of the things I had said, marking him arrogant or just acknowledging my status. That didn't stop me from proceeding. "Might you deliver a message on my behalf in exchange for your favor?"

"A message to Birk?"

I nodded. "I would dearly love to let my parents know I am safe." Waving a hand at the buzzing room, I added, "Or at least still breathing."

"And how do you propose I get this message all the way to Central?" His voice was infinitely colder now, but most nobles took requests as an affront so his attitude didn't deter me.

"My mother often has conversations with the castle's bird messengers. Or even the flocks of sparrows and finches would do, although I would imagine those would be quite beneath you." And such small birds probably served as supper for him a good deal of the time.

"The castle has several hunting birds that could hold the information until asked as well. Then too, my parents may be enroute. I'm sure you could convince—"

"You dare such an insult?!? Do I look like a lowly, caught messenger bird to you?"

I tilted my head. His tone had my fingers itching towards my dagger. "Insult? You just asked me to deliver a message. An even exchange, I would think."

Star appeared next to me, her claws skidding on the stone floor. She sat and let her tongue hang out. I decided it was time to stand, even though the bird-man would still be above me. Derrick was shifting through the crowds on his way to us.

I waited until Derrick took up residence on my other side before responding to the hawk. "Well, I suppose it is too late to obtain a valuable favor now. You can inform Derrick yourself about the meeting tomorrow at the noon roost."

"Favor," Derrick repeated in a flat tone, folding his arms across his chest.

I nodded. "Shae didn't wish to let any of the birds in Birk know that I was still breathing. Seemed a simple enough request to me, but apparently too much trouble for one of his import."

Derrick's eyes darted away from Shae long enough to glance at me. Then he outright chuckled. "Ah, Shae." He stopped to laugh harder. Shae began to bristle again, his feathers standing out and the hair on the base of his neck more like quills dragged down by long hair on the ends.

"Your charge had best watch her welcome," Shae snapped.

Derrick waved a hand, but his smile didn't disappear. "She talks to birds all the time, Shae. I've seen her do it, and I doubt she meant any insult. I swear she might have stood there telling the finches her life story had I not interrupted."

"Finches?" Shae's claws again contracted, an obvious threat.

Derrick nodded. "If she asked you to deliver a message via birds, she wouldn't see it as an insult."

I interrupted the exchange. "It's an insult? You mean to tell me he can't do it? Oh. Well, I had no idea. I just assumed"

Derrick reached over, wrapped his arm around me and put his hand over my mouth. I didn't appreciate the gesture, but since survival seemed more likely with me quiet, I just glared silently. Derrick did not remove his hand even after I stopped speaking, which annoyed me further.

He said, "She informed me of how glad she was to see I was able to keep chickens without eating them outright."

That had not been what I said at all.

Shae stared coldly at us, probably gauging whether he could claw both of our eyes out at the same time.

Derrick nodded. "She didn't see that as an insult either and mentioned how much she liked chicken sausage."

Shae blinked, something that a hunting bird probably didn't do often when he had prey in sight. Slowly, he scratched his chin. Finally, he asked, "Do the birds answer her?"

Derrick started to reply, but then hesitated. "I don't know." He looked down at me, but his hand still covered my mouth. Very slowly, very deliberately, I licked his hand from one side of my lips to the other.

He was a warrior through and through. No reaction showed on his face, but his fingers did spasm once.

Since both men were still watching me and waiting, I licked my lips again. This time, Derrick took the hint and released me. "Of course they do," I said.

"And you understand them?"

This scrutiny was really much deeper than necessary. "Given that I just asked you to deliver a message via birds to my mother, do you really think I meant for you to have the bird draw out the letters in a sandbox and wait for her to read them?" Star moved in front of my hand to divert attention away from the fact that I was using the dress pocket to replace my knife back in its hidden sheath now that the tension had ratcheted down a notch. "Of course, you could have just written out a message and delivered it using the leg bands on the messenger birds. Was that too much to ask? Or are you telling me you don't use messenger birds at all?"

"We use them. But that is not what you asked."

"Well, of course not; they aren't very efficient. The messenger birds stop several times, half the messages get dropped, changed or outright stolen. I thought you might have a more reliable system that would ensure my parents would actually receive the message. Especially if my parents are traveling."

The bird-man blinked again. Slowly. "I still don't see how I'm not supposed to be insulted."

Derrick squeezed my shoulder. "She grows on you."

Shae gave a wheezing snort that sounded like a half squawk. "On some. Perhaps. Consider my message delivered." He dipped his head at me. "I'll give some thought to yours." With a whisper of feathers, he changed and launched himself from the platform.

Derrick relaxed infinitesimally. "I've been meaning to tell you that treating shifters as animals will get you killed."

I pushed my hair over my shoulder and wished for my braids. "Can he talk to birds or not?"

Derrick sighed. "Yes, of course."

"And he's insulted by that."

"No, of course not."

Star leaned against my leg. I wasn't sure if she was telling me to be quiet or showing me support. She seemed to be laughing, her tongue lolling about and her eyes wobbling from side to side as if they might fall right out of her head at any moment. "I don't get it."

"It's complicated. Animals have a hierarchy that humans do not. We're equal as humans, but in the animal world it cannot be so. Reminders of our different natures is seen as a challenge. Bringing up a strength or weakness in conversation is only done as a veiled threat or reference to an implied weakness."

"But I *like* animals!" I shook my head. "You don't make any sense."

Derrick sighed. "Neither do you. Time to go. None of this is going to be any more logical in the morning, but we've been given a reprieve to prove we can rescue Lindis."

Derrick wouldn't answer why it was our job to rescue her and not the dragons' job, but I knew the answer: Politics. Everyone would be looking for her; she was still a prize. Even under the spell of the ring, most would want her. If they couldn't control her or gain her favor they'd just kill her off.

The dragons were busy arguing over whether Lindis had been fairly won by Anton or since magic was obviously used and against the rules, she had to be retrieved even at the cost of war. Lindis had been right about the auction, but she had downplayed the fact that several dragons had fully intended to choose her suitor and thus position themselves in the ranks. It was no surprise that the humans in any territory hadn't been considered as possible contenders.

It was almost three in the morning when we finally arrived at Derrick's cottage. I was exhausted, barely hanging onto Hewitt and a borrowed crystal lantern. My eyes were not like those of the wolves. I required light, especially carrying Hewitt.

Derrick and his father stayed deep in conversation the entire way back. Star and her mother continued on past the cottage without stopping, but Derrick's father paused.

"I don't believe we've been properly introduced," he said as I was about to disappear inside with Hewitt. Hewitt made himself a very obvious presence by staying right next to me even after I put him down. "Go inside and wash up," I told him. "I'll get some food for us in a bit."

He didn't move other than to peer around my leg.

Well, at least we had established who was boss. "Zoe, from Central," I said on a sigh. "This is Hewitt."

Derrick said, "Yes, this is the long-lost Hewitt, son of the gryphon who was running Gorgon University and who most recently did his level best to destroy the dragon's lair. Quite a reputation his son will have to live up to."

Derrick's father held out a hand. I shook it. "Seth. Perhaps we should hold the child hostage until he and his confess the names of those working with the gryphon. He could be a valuable commodity to those shuffling for position. Or maybe he can somehow be traded for Lindis."

Lack of sleep or perhaps sheer stupidity made me panic. I pushed Hewitt's head firmly behind me and shook my crystal lantern at Seth because I didn't have a free hand to go for my knife. "He had nothing to do with the gryphon! He's mine, and you can't have him for your political games!"

Derrick raised his eyebrows, and the gold in his eyes flickered against the dim light.

"I changed my mind," I told him. "Hewitt is my cub."

"Changed your mind? I don't think it works that way."

I kept my hand on Hewitt so that the little seer would stay behind me just in case he had other ideas. "He's mine, and you cannot use him," I said stubbornly.

Derrick folded his arms across his broad chest and stared down at me. "And who is his father?"

I straightened my back and huffed in a deep breath to answer. The only problem was that I hadn't thought of an answer. "Um." I didn't dare lower my gaze. "Not the gryphon," I declared rashly.

Hewitt pushed his fist into the air. "Not the gryphon!" he agreed happily.

I looked down at him in surprise. "Really? Are you sure?" On second thought, my eyes flew to Derrick's, but he was grinning, not fooled in the first place.

Hewitt said, "He hides his gryphon, and doesn't talk about it ever. Mama said he was ours. Not from Wendal anymore. We ate a lot more after he came." His eyes were too sad and knowledgeable for a four year old.

"See," I told Derrick triumphantly. "Not the gryphon!"

"Uh-huh. Okay. Not the gryphon. Father was not serious about holding him hostage."

Seth was displaying a quite ominous frown that implied he might be insulted.

"Oh."

"Oh, indeed," Seth said softly. "Get inside then. Your cub is safe."

I didn't need the invitation twice. As I closed the door behind me, he said, "She's a little thing until she gets mad, isn't she?"

Derrick apparently wasn't quite finished talking, which left me time to get Hewitt cleaned, fed some cheese and tucked into the blankets. While I was showering, Derrick came in and started dinner.

When I stepped into the main room, the smell of grilled meat filled the air.

"Eggs too?" I asked.

"Too dark to find."

"I'll watch the meat if you want to clean up."

"And recharge your crystals? We're going to need them to get Lindis back." On his way past, he stopped and found my hand. He held it silently for a moment, but then lifted it to his lips. A smile glinted in his eyes, but instead of running his tongue across it, he kissed it. "You smell good," he said.

I opened my mouth to answer, but I had none. The room was very hot from the fire.

He stepped away and shut the door to the bathing room. "Don't let the meat burn," he called from within.

The kitchen was too small and very warm. I cooked. Derrick's mother had left cheese and bread...how long ago had it been since we went to the auction?

By the time Derrick was out of the shower, I had stacked giant sandwiches of steaming meat and cheese. I made him three and one for me, setting aside some of the bread and cheese for Hewitt when he woke up.

By the time I finished eating, sleep nearly owned me. Derrick stood at the doorway, ready to do his perimeter check. He stared at Hewitt thoughtfully before his eyes drifted to me. "I'll stay wolf tonight," he said. "Safer."

"Probably a good idea," I said, a mixture of relief and...anxiety.

"Can you find her?" he asked quietly.

"If she drops the tracking protection we set."

"Can you bring her back?"

"I don't know. The spell for that requires both dragon and woman because she is both. If I set the spell for those things, I might get the ring. I might get her. I might get nothing at all."

His eyes drifted to Hewitt again. "He might be more comfortable with my family than here. And more protected too if we have to track Lindis."

I avoided his gaze, but could feel the heat of it anyway. "Hewitt has a habit of showing up where he wants to be. Seers are like that." I chanced a peek. Derrick's beautiful eyes lacked any yellow of his wolf, but somehow he was all wolf, all predator, watching, waiting. One word of encouragement and Derrick...what? I blinked and shook myself. We were of two very different worlds.

This was Wendal. I didn't belong here. We both knew it. But for just a moment, I thought he might want me here. For something other than the job of keeping Wendal free of interfering mages and kings. I sighed. "It would have been a lot better if you had found a real mage."

"We'll see," he said softly.

I headed for the blankets.

The door clicked behind him.

Chapter 15 — Dragon Rage

Lindis choked on a scream. *Spawn of a three-eyed goat!* Rage burned next to desperation, but even as the man called Camden from Anton grabbed her up, she fought. His touch freed her from whatever had frozen her, and she didn't need to be dragon to kill.

The nauseating shift of being transported wasn't new to her either, thanks to Lonnie. She ignored her stomach and gouged at Camden's eyes, twisting his head back and sideways. "You don't want that ring," she hissed.

He was weak. The landing sent her sprawling away, but she lunged for him even faster than he came after her. The scents of old campfire, forest, fear and sweat separated themselves into categories on her second breath. He was drenched with the fear and sweat, but instead of grabbing for his weapons, he wrapped her in one meaty arm only to immediately fling her away again.

As she smashed into the ground, she felt the bands of magic flare around her. Instead of rolling away, she slammed into an invisible barrier.

Caged!

The warrior thief from Anton collapsed, nearly erasing links that had apparently been set and waiting for her.

Lindis wasted precious energy hurling herself against the magic circle. The cage was barely large enough to contain her had she been dragon. In her human form she had room to lunge end to end, but it was to no avail.

Red-hot coals burned in her stomach, and the tips of her ears were hot from steam. She smelled the comforting presence of sulfur.

Sulfur? *Heat??*

Her dragon was not entirely gone this time!

The ring that had stolen her inner beast, her sense of being, her very self...was not completely missing. She was not a baby wren, injured and bleeding, with none of her dragon sense. No, this time...she breathed deep and felt the coals of her rage crackle deep in her belly. Her head was nicely warm and...*yes!* She flexed her fingers, fingers that contained talons. Their solid, unbending strength was there, but not quite within reach. It was...almost...

She smiled and felt the tips of very sharp teeth. The spell was weakened. Perhaps it was because of the death of the gryphon or as the little mage had taught, perhaps the magic needed to be reset. "It will never get the chance," she promised.

First things first. The cage contained a rough bedroll and a packet of dried meat at one end. She used the moth-eaten wool blanket as a cape. She didn't care about her nakedness, but the cape was useful for fighting and for keeping the little mage's yellow crystal hidden. She reached for her necklace and released the spell that protected her from being tracked and transported. "Now, little mage friend, find me."

Surely the girl was smart enough. Then again...the little mage had better not try to transport her back. The very idea made Lindis nervous. There was no point in being transported without the ring. The damn ring. Was it safer to keep the protection up so that Zoe didn't accidentally drag her further from the ring?

Lindis fingered the crystal. She needed the energy it contained for other things. Where else could she obtain magical energy? The fire on the far side of the camp had been covered and was outside her reach in any case.

As she searched her surroundings, she smiled. It was not her human eyes that picked things out of the dark. No, it was her dragon sight that was working perfectly. The spell was weakened indeed.

She tested her sense of smell again, quickly discerning the odor of the dried meat inside the cage. She could pick out Camden's location with her nose and find where he had relieved himself hours before. Yes, she could smell much, but she couldn't smell magic. Or could she?

The glyphs of her cage were invisible, sparking to light only when she slammed into them. She sniffed along the edges. There was rich earth, the scent of decaying leaves...she pulled her dragon as close to the surface as she could. There was a sense of something of the man who set the spell, of Camden.

That the dried meat and waterskin also smelled of him proved nothing. The tang of smoke on the food could be from the drying process or...was it some spell set for dragons? A call to keep her fire contained? But she wasn't dragon now and the man who kidnapped her didn't expect her to be able to become one.

She couldn't see the glyphs, but she knew the glyph for dragons, including the one the little mage had shown her on the inside of the ring.

Lindis stroked the yellow crystal. It retained the energy stored there. What if she drew the glyph for her dragon? Could it call her dragon closer?

She stared outside her boundary at the man lying in a heap. He was clearly visible to her even though the night held no moon.

Dragon. She had part of her dragon.

Only a few scant inches separated her from Camden. Just those few kept him breathing. She licked her lips, hungry for the kill, for freedom, for justice.

She held the crystal and drew the glyph. She gave it a word of power.

She held her breath, but nothing happened. Her dragon was still restless, wanting to be free. Maybe the crystal didn't retain enough energy. The campfire was too far to be of any use in gaining more.

The crystal rolled in her fingers as she stroked the planes and edges. Lonnie didn't use crystals to fuel his spells. Zoe had told her it was possible to use oneself for energy, but dangerous. So was being trapped inside glyphs by a madman.

If the crystal needed fire, she knew just where to get some.

The flames in her belly roared.

She pulled and directed...*steam?*

Disgust nearly made her give up. "Nothing but heated vapor?" It would take hours to charge the crystal that way.

But steam was more than she had had before. If she spent her time storing dragon fire now, she'd have the energy in the crystal for later.

Chapter 16 — The Wolf Glen

I was a quiet sleeper and Derrick's pallet of blankets was longer and larger than I needed. Hewitt had no real reason to seek out Derrick, but when I woke after only three hours of sleep, he was curled up next to the wolf on the stone floor. A wispy impression of a kiss on my forehead right before I slept had me touching my face, but there was no evidence it had been anything more than a dream.

The wolf, eyes closed, guarded the front door. One giant paw rested over Hewitt's small shoulders. If the wolf rolled over, Hewitt would be buried.

Neither seemed concerned about the possibility. Hewitt was curled under the wolf's paw as if he had slept with a breathing fur blanket his entire life.

It was too early for breakfast, but not too early to make an attempt to discover where Lindis might have been taken. Yawning, I washed up and took myself outside. Hewitt didn't wake, but the wolf's golden eyes watched me slip out the back door.

My white crystal was tight in my fist, fully charged from resting in the stove overnight. My other arm cradled cousin Lonnie's book of spells.

A tracking spell for Lindis wouldn't be too difficult, but a scrying spell would be more useful. The white crystal was far too cloudy to be an ideal scrying tool, but it could provide the power needed. If there had been time to make friends with the birds here, they might also have been of use to me. I talked to them anyway as I arranged an area by the stream to work.

Water was good for scrying. With part of the glyph over the water, the reflective surface would be good for details.

I didn't see the hawk arrive, probably because he didn't want to be seen. When he finally hopped into the tree near my work area, there was no mistaking him as ordinary. He was twice as large as any normal hawk, and his eyes were unforgettably intelligent.

He changed, but this time he did it as he was on his way to the ground. His feathers remained again, but his feet and wings completely disappeared. "You do talk to them."

"Shae," I greeted him. "Yes. I'm hopeful they will send word of

Lindis just by happenstance. Can't hurt to tell them what to look for."

"Why not negotiate with me to help find her? Wouldn't that favor be easier than requesting I find people completely unknown to me in order to deliver a message?"

"Depends on where Lindis is being held. Above ground? Below? Anton? Wendal? I assume you're looking for her anyway. Why should I waste a favor?"

His eyes were reddish-brown even in his human form. It could be that, like the feathers, he didn't change them over. Exchanging the accuracy and distance ability of the hawk's eyes for the lesser ability of human ones wouldn't be all that enticing a prospect, especially for one with his personality.

"Are you claimed?" Shae asked abruptly. "By the wolf or the mage who dropped in from the ceiling during the dragon's ball?"

My eyes narrowed. "You mean Derrick?" I had no intention of naming cousin Lonnie. He was a problem, and he might indeed try to claim me for various purposes, but that was no business of this nosy bird.

"Or anyone else, for that matter?"

"Yes."

There was a long silence between us.

His forehead lifted when it became obvious I was not going to elaborate. His lack of eyebrows didn't detract from the handsome angles of his face, but it made him more birdlike. "That is too bad. I would have liked you to meet my son."

It was easy to forget my manners in the face of his confident supremacy, but my mother hadn't drilled court customs into Lonnie for naught. "It would be too great an honor for one such as myself in any case." I lowered my eyes briefly in lieu of a courtly bow, which wasn't possible since I was already kneeling in order to draw the glyphs over the water.

He dipped his head in acknowledgment. "Even so." He changed on his way back to the sky.

Watching the muscles in his legs bunch and flex and the sheer power that such a move required left me in awe even though he was overbearing. My eyes tracked the path of the bird up and away. What was it like to catch the breeze and fly?

I shook my head and turned back to my glyphs. If scrying didn't work...even if it did, it would use up energy in the crystal. There wouldn't be enough power left to attempt a transport spell. The white was the only crystal I trusted to contain enough energy to bring Lindis through. After all, it had ported Derrick, myself and Lonnie.

I could ask Lonnie for advice, but he wouldn't be any real help. He tended to put energy haphazardly into his glyphs and then if more was needed, he fed it from himself. Idiot.

"Progress?"

I jumped, but stopped short of spinning around to ward off an attack. "Must you sneak up on me?" I complained.

"I stood here for a long time waiting for you to notice me." Derrick managed to sound insulted.

I ignored his hurt. "I'm trying to decide whether to try a transport spell or a scrying spell. Or a tracking spell. If Lindis and her captor are nearby, the tracking spell makes the most sense. If not, the transport spell. But since I don't know anything at all, maybe the scrying spell is best."

"Did you leave home because you're betrothed to your cousin Lonnie, and you refused the alliance?"

"What?" My hand faltered and smashed right through the glyph I had just drawn. I shot to my feet and faced him. His eyes were all human, but they had a slightly wild look as though he had recently changed and kept the wolf at the surface.

"Are you crazed? Betrothed? I'd have done more than leave Central! His parents may have talked my parents into training him for the court, but if they had *dared* suggest...well, for that matter, his family thinks we're quite beneath them, most especially me, I'm certain." I glanced back down at my glyphs in dismay, unclenching my fists. Talk of being betrothed to Lonnie was enough to make me reach for my dagger. On top of that, this whole "rescue Lindis" idea was very troubling.

"Now look what you've done," I sighed. Not that I had decided what to do, but the basics had been drawn. "I'll have to start over. I can't risk messing up a spell when I've never even tried it before."

Derrick was not contrite. He crossed his arms, making it clear he was affronted, about to berate me for something or challenge someone.

"What? Do you think there's a better spell?" I asked.

"If not Lonnie then who? Hewitt is not your son. So who has a claim on you?"

"Derrick, what are you going on about—were you standing there when Shae flew by?"

"This is my territory. Little happens here without me knowing about it. Shae is well aware of that fact. My hearing is quite good."

I blinked. "Oh. Well. Of course."

"Who?" His voice was dangerously quiet, much like at the dance when he thought the gryphon had not properly claimed me.

I raised my chin. "Me."

"Yes, who has a claim on you?" he repeated.

I pointed to my chest. "Me. I have my own claim. I'm not a noble to be bargained, auctioned or given away because some lofty hawk shifter finds it interesting that I chat with birds. What is the point of being lowborn if you end up traded like a noble? If he's looking for a chess piece, he can go after Lindis. He'd be mighty disappointed the day he discovered I'm not even a half-mage and useless to him. Then what would happen? I'd end up in a dungeon asked to do spells to earn less than a basic meal!" I stomped my foot. "I'll not have it. He can go find a noble and play his games. I need to become a mage and get myself a real position."

Derrick's frown deepened, forming lines across his forehead. "You lied? You can't go around telling people you are claimed if you are not."

"I told you! I am claimed."

"He wasn't asking to use you as a chess piece. He was asking permission for his son to court you. It's how it is done."

"That's not at all the way it sounded, and I don't care what he thinks. I claim me for me." I folded my own arms, glowering at least as stubbornly as Derrick.

"Shae isn't—" He stopped as though considering his words carefully. "You can't—well, you just did." He eyed me up and down, his disapproval changing to a smile. "You're right. You don't have to answer to him. I'm sure his son won't mind."

"Rules," I muttered. I only need to know enough rules to survive. And I wasn't very good at those, either. "I am definitely *not* betrothed to Lonnie!"

"Good."

"I need to figure out this spell." Wendal and Lindis needed more than a half-mage. Calling myself that was being generous. I was more like a one-trick pony.

A small face appeared from behind the side of a giant oak tree. Hewitt's hand held a gold clip, one that had been in my dress pocket the last time I had seen it.

"Hewitt! What are you doing with that?" When he didn't answer immediately, I guessed. "Are you suggesting I transport Camden the warrior here using that clip? I don't know if I can hold him. He's a far better mage than I am."

Hewitt smiled and shook his head. He trotted over, handing me the gold clasp. I didn't like touching it. The owner was an evil man.

"Those and this." He drew a pattern in the sandy bank. "That inside this."

"Hewitt, the glyphs have to be exactly right. Can you draw the whole thing?"

He shook his head. "Not me. Never magic."

Uh-oh. "Can you tell if I get it exactly right?"

He smiled. "You draw."

"Here," I shoved the book at Derrick. "Look up the glyph he just drew. See if you can find it." I got to drawing, adding my glyphs in the sand next to his.

"Not in the center," he said. "It goes in the glyph."

"The clip?" I moved it to his glyph.

"NO. Never use mine. You draw it."

Arguing with a four-year-old was hopeless. "I don't think I've ever put anything of a person's inside a glyph itself. Inside the circle of all the glyphs, yes." So what would it do? What was the difference? "I don't think the book covers that."

Derrick didn't stop searching the pages, regardless. The spells were cross referenced by shapes, by intent, and also by complexity. Finding one symbol and a complex one at that...he'd never find it.

"Okay, like this?" I set the clip in the sand and drew his glyph around it. Then I began setting the basic glyphs to tie it to magic.

"Your crystal not inside. Outside."

"I can use it from outside the glyphs, but to do what?" I usually held the crystal over the glyphs or inside the pentagram of glyphs. Sometimes it was part of the spell, and sometimes it was merely for storing energy.

Hewitt kept his eyes on the circle, so I started to draw again. The crystal was not set to do anything specific, and the clip being a part of the circle meant nothing to me. Would this spell call the power from the crystal to the clip?

No, the clip wasn't a focus, it was a part of the drawing itself. I had no idea what I was doing. This was worse than working with Lonnie. The only difference was that Lonnie was an idiot, and Hewitt was a seer. I wasn't sure it was an improvement.

I finished the basic circle, but there wasn't much to it.

"Now this inside." Hewitt drew three glyphs. They were extremely complex, and at least one of them contained the symbol for a dragon.

The other had the symbol for a lady, just as I had used to keep Lonnie or anyone else from tracking Lindis. "The end goes here." He pointed to the gold clip. "The top two not touch."

I gave a desperate sigh. "I sure hope you know what I'm doing."

The end result was a "Y" shape with the gold clip across the top, inside the first glyph. The "Y" reminded me of a gutter with the crystal as a bucket underneath.

My circle would do nothing but tie it all to the crystal. The "Y" wasn't large enough to contain anything, which was a good thing because if Camden showed up here, I'd need a lot more than this tiny circle to hold him. Even though Hewitt didn't suggest it, I drew the mute symbols and set it to the blue crystal. It might not save us. If the warrior-mage had his immobilization spell ready to go, we'd be in real trouble.

"Derrick, it might be a good idea if you stayed hidden like when you sneak up on me."

"I don't sneak up on you!"

Hewitt said, "Connect those lines. Pull the power to the crystal."

I blinked. "The crystal already has power in it. I pulled fire into it when we got home."

He pressed his lips together and waited. It wasn't quite a pout, but almost.

"Fine, fine. You're the mage." I set it up as he described. The symbols to draw and contain power didn't need to be in the sand. I could draw and erase them in my sleep. But what was I calling this time? Camden's power wasn't going to be contained inside one tiny crystal! So...I looked again at the Y. It was two gutters running down into a container. Hmm. But what was I draining and from where? And would the crystal contain it or overflow?

As soon as I was finished, Hewitt clapped. "Okay, done. Call it!"

Derrick gripped my shoulders. "I think I'll stand right here." He was holding me hard enough that if I was somehow sucked away, he'd go with me.

Hewitt, on the other hand, wasn't the least bit worried. He clapped again. "Call it!"

I looked to Derrick for reassurance. My hesitation was too long and gave him ideas. He crouched down next to me, shifting his hold to tuck me under one arm. "You're right. I'll do it."

"No, you won't!" We grabbed the white at the same time. He only knew one of my words of Power. We yelled it together.

Chapter 17 — Dragon Revenge

Lindis was tempted by the dried meat, but it was smarter to shut down into dormancy and reserve her energy rather than eat what might be food tainted by magic. At this point, going full dragon wasn't possible, but that didn't mean she couldn't attain the same resting state. If she could breathe enough steam to power the crystal, she was close enough to dragon to do many dragon things.

She rested thus until shards of sunlight broke through the branches. The rising sun hit the patch where she was caged and, half dozing, she flicked to scales. The back of her neck changed, waking her fully.

Aaah. Scales loved sunlight. Warmth that regenerated the fire in her belly. She tested a talon again. Yes, she was definitely stronger than the last time. The tip of her finger sharpened; the fingernail hardened and lengthened. Even better than last night. Whatever spell was on that ring had weakened greatly with the death of one of its masters.

All she had to do was get free of this cage. She eyed her tormentor, who was still prone on the ground. Muddy locks of brown hair were weighted with sweat, blood and filth. The wind snared the occasional piece, showing a not unhandsome face, but not a terribly young one either. Where the gryphon had been much more aged, this man was maybe forty or forty-five human years. Callouses had earned a spot on his hands, and his boots were well-worn.

"Why would a mage such as yourself tie himself to the debt of a gryphon?"

He mumbled an answer or threat when her voice penetrated his slogged brain.

She hadn't expected a response. Since collapsing, he hadn't moved. There was no way to know how long it would take for him to regain consciousness. The little mage, Zoe, had explained that Lonnie expended himself on a regular basis, but Lindis had not asked how long it took for him to recover. If Lonnie had never recovered it would have been little more than a curiosity to her, but she found her previous lack of interest was now a source of frustration.

Camden-SoonToDie rolled over and groaned.

Lindis did not stir. She sank further into dragon rest, pulling the comfort to her. Obviously she needed to fool this creature into opening the cage or canceling it entirely. How best to accomplish that? The little mage excelled at fooling her opponents. So small and helpless, she seemed. Her face was always blank, her crystals hidden. You never saw the dagger she carried until she was ready and willing to use it.

Sweet-natured then. No, Zoe was not really sweet. She was quiet; subdued at times to avoid being noticed. Zoe kept her head down so that the threat in her eyes could not be seen. She spouted polite nonsense as though repeating something she had heard often, sounding almost sincere and very proper, like a well-schooled child. And since she looked close enough to a child, it was believable.

Lindis yawned and felt her teeth. They were proper and sharp, dragon's teeth. They were still short, but they were dragon weapons.

She was not a little mage. She would rather let her prey know exactly what would happen to him and how. Yes, she was dragon and this man would dream of his death before it visited. She would not cower in the corner or pretend.

Standing, she gripped the crystal. It now had the power of dragon heat. She could reach nothing outside the cage, but she could work with what was inside. She knew the dragon glyph, and she knew the calling from Lonnie's pentagram.

Drawing the glyphs, she hoped the spell would pull more of the dragon essence that was bound to the ring back to herself. She gave it a single dragon-word, one that a human could not hope to pronounce.

The snap of magic flashed across her skin.

She smiled. The result was enough that she clothed herself in the scales that she loved and craved. She stoked the fire in her belly and felt the glow of dragon in her eyes. She loosed the crystal from her neck and carefully sketched the charging glyphs she had learned from the little mage. Let the crystal draw and store the power of the sun now.

Turning to her prey, she hissed, "If you let me go now, your death will be quick. If you linger over your decision, so will I linger over your pain."

His head jerked up, meeting the wrath of dragon eyes. Discovering that he was no more than two strides away from such a threatening beast, he forgot himself.

"Aaagh!"

For a scant moment, Lindis could tell he didn't remember the cage. When he did, he rolled to a sitting position, but did no more than breathe hard and stare.

"It would seem you wanted a dragon." Lindis deliberately let smoke curl around her words. "Now you have one." She crossed an arm in front of herself and raised her other hand to stare at him over one stunted talon. It was half its normal size, but sharp enough. "Did you really think we could mate and live happily ever after?" She deliberately rippled the scales that showed across her arms. The sunlight caught and reflected each one a thousand times over.

"You—you're changed." He immediately snatched the ring from his finger, holding it to the light of morning.

"It has lost its magic. You cannot change what I am. Even if the magic still worked, I would soon wrestle my dragon free. Your plans would crumple to dust like you humans do after only a few years." It had felt like death, being without her dragon. She would not go there again, but her tormentor would.

"Damn the gryphon!"

"Are you not a mage?" Lindis asked. "The great mage who worked the magic of the ring?"

He tapped on the sapphire. "The blood of the dragon hasn't been breached." He frowned over the ring and drew a glyph over its surface. The glyph he drew was invisible, but another glyph appeared above the ring in a fiery blue. It held for a moment and then faded. A red dot balanced in the center of the symbol, the one Zoe had said was a dragon glyph.

Lindis already knew that glyph, but not the one he had drawn to make it appear as a blue glow. Luckily, Camden-SoonToDie drew the first glyph several more times. Each time he formed the pattern, a new line of visible glyphs glowed in the air, piling one atop the other like a scroll. "Too complex. He added...he tied himself to the ring!"

There was another dot inside a different symbol, one Lindis was willing to bet was that of a gryphon.

Camden-SoonToDie sketched in the air again, but this time, instead of more symbols, he got sparks that didn't form full lines. He swore. "I'll read them, bastard lion!" His fingers formed the pattern again with a slight modification.

Lindis made note of his attempt, but his new design didn't change the results. Nothing but sparks filled the air.

Sweat broke across his brow as he tried again and again, producing faint dots of light like dying fireflies.

Lindis stored the symbols, watching and biding her time. No one was more patient than a dragon waiting on prey. "It seems the gryphon never intended to turn me over to you and yours. Will you now try your own blood? Do you think it will be enough to bind me even though you can't read the entire spell?" She showed a lot of teeth when she asked.

"You'd be bound to the prince already if it wasn't for that interfering half-wit girl."

"Then it was the king of Anton who asked you to find a dragon for his son? Who will die first if you deliver me and I'm not properly bound?" Lindis belched smoke to bring her point home. "Your life will not be worth much."

"What human would want you?" he sneered. "You're nothing but an overgrown lizard."

"Someone wanted me married to the prince of Anton."

Camden paced, his attention riveted on the ring. "We wanted Anton by the balls. If we controlled you and you were married to Irwin, we controlled Anton. The gryphon *promised*." He spit and glared at her. "The prince would have been forced to grant me the title of Wizard of Anton. He would have done whatever we demanded in order to stay alive."

Lindis laughed, softly at first and then roared. All this time she had thought herself the big prize. But this mage had really wanted control of Anton and a lofty position. Ah, ego. "And the gryphon? Did he plan to control Wendal as well or just start a war?"

But Camden wasn't listening to her. He was more interested in his own muttering. "You'll be the great mage you were meant to be, he said. You'll be the Wizard of Anton and those who laughed before will rue the day. Until the bastard gryphon decided he had learned enough of *my spells*." He cursed, spittle spewing from his lips. "Dragon's blood...The glyphs were the right ones...why did he use his own blood?!?" Camden rubbed his face, smearing the dirt there.

He tried to read the spells on the ring again, but the glyphs sputtered to a stop in the same place as before.

If he wasn't already physically ill, he was working his way there.

Lindis said, "You may as well release me." She stretched a talon in his direction and they both watched it grow, snapping into place. "With a little more time, I'll be dragon again." He didn't need to know that she let go of the scales on her back to force the talon. She could shift. But only partially and it was far more work than it should have been.

He was mesmerized by the sharp length of her talon. She wiggled it and began to grow another.

"Time..." He held the ring up again. "I could redo the ring."

She needed to keep him distracted or panicked. The crystal wouldn't have much sunlight stored yet, but all she required was a temporary diversion. She picked up the yellow crystal and drew a circle inside the border of her cage. At the end, she sketched the reveal glyph that SoonToDie had just used over and over.

Just as the glyph had revealed the spells used on the ring, it now lit up the glyphs he had drawn to form the magical cage that held her captive. "Ah magic." The little mage would be proud. Lindis memorized the cage glyphs, even as she sent a silent thanks to Zoe for teaching her the basics.

Camden-SoonToDie cursed. "Your clan will pay to get you back! I will still be a rich man."

She ignored his screaming as she set the yellow to again draw power from the sun. It took her several minutes to realize he was packing and preparing to depart.

"Will you leave me to starve?" she asked, not worried about food in the least. The ring departing the vicinity, however, was a different problem.

"The gryphon's wife will negotiate with your dragon elders for your freedom," he said. "She had better. Or you will starve. If you happen to escape before then, it won't be my problem."

"Coward!"

He turned back at the last minute, gripping the pommel of his sword, his eyes narrowing in thought. "They don't know if you are dead or alive. They'll assume you are alive. They will negotiate in any case, and I'm better off without an enemy at my back."

Lindis raised a talon. "See if that sword is long enough to reach me." *And break the glyphs.* He had drawn them. If he crossed them, they would fall. She could withstand a slice against her scales long enough to gain the advantage. One strike would be all he'd get.

He drew the sword and stalked the length of the cage while he tried to make up his mind.

Lindis pushed dragon scales across the important places; her throat, her right arm, her heart and stomach. Adrenaline or the fact that the ring was closer made it easier. She could smell his fear, the sick-sweet of old sweat mixed with new, and the splash of gryphon blood across his clothes. Swirling around his human stink was another smell, that of...spent magic.

Camden-SoonToDie flexed and raised the sword with both hands.

A battering slash then. She waited as closely as possible near the edge of the cage. She hardened her scales. She might bleed, but she would not die.

The swirling cage glyphs she had called to light had faded to bare wisps. There was nothing but open space for him to cross, until, with a strange popping sound, the symbols of the cage flared again. Then, with a faint slurp, they melted down to the ground and disappeared.

Like a wind that had gone instantly still, the pressure against Lindis' skin was gone.

SoonToDie felt the magic disperse. His eyes widened and his sword jerked.

Lindis did not hesitate. She was light and fast and in her current form, small enough to slide by his open side, her talons stabbing and cutting.

She turned before he began the swing back. It was only a matter of bleeding him out.

Chapter 18 — The Wolf Glen

Derrick had me tucked so closely under his arm, my neck was bent at an awkward angle. The crystal flashed once and went from cloudy white to an odd soured milk color. The center smudge was surrounded by an even muddier yellow brown.

"What happened?" Derrick asked.

I peered closer. The crystal had stopped changing colors. It didn't explode, roll away or do anything else abnormal. I poked at it with one finger. "It stored something. Energy probably."

"Is it safe?"

"I've never pulled energy to a crystal in that manner. I always pull energy from light, cold or fire. It's easier to do a spell if I happen to use a like energy on the way back out. For example, energy stored from fire uses less of it to start my campfire than if the energy originally came from cold. But the energy can be changed by the glyphs so the original type isn't crucial."

Derrick shifted from his crouch to a seated position, but instead of releasing me, he moved his arm from crushing my shoulders to circling my waist. "So can you use it?"

"I guess." Our heads swiveled to Hewitt.

He smiled at us with bright brown eyes. "Let's go to mama now." He reached up and flexed his fingers into a fist and then expanded his fingers again.

"What does that mean?" Derrick asked.

My head was inches from Derrick's. It was very tempting to lean into him and rest against his chest. I held very still and didn't stop watching Hewitt, but I did take a deep breath. Derrick always smelled like the forest; a mix of tree bark baking in the sunshine with just a hint of cinnamon. Unintentionally, I relaxed into his side. I hadn't had nearly enough sleep, and if I sat here too long, I would drift off. Probably.

"Did we help Lindis?" I asked Hewitt.

He nodded.

"Shouldn't we do more? Like maybe scry to see where she is at?"

Hewitt shrugged. "Mama misses me."

I sighed. "Is it okay if we eat first? Do you know where your mother is?"

Hewitt smiled. "When the dragons come, we go. At the gryphon place."

My back straightened so quickly, my head nearly took out Derrick's chin. The second I turned, his brown and gold eyes caught my wide and worried ones.

"Anywhere but the gryphons," he groaned.

"Dragons and gryphons? Didn't the dragons just jail the two highest ranking gryphons at the ball last night?" Sitting this close to Derrick, there really was no need to yell.

"Yes. And gryphons and dragons are always dangerous. They are the two strongest clans in Wendal." He stared down at me. His free hand slowly reached up to my jawline. "Zoe, when this is over...where do you plan to go?"

Before an answer was even possible, he muttered, "To hell with it," and kissed me anyway, right in front of Hewitt, the bright blue sky and...a large crashing beast that took out at least one tree branch on the way down.

It is nearly impossible to roll from a sitting position with someone kissing you. I tried to go one way, but Derrick was stronger, so we went the other way. I had my dagger somewhere...boot, yes it was in my boot, which was attached to...I was flat on my back staring up at Derrick who had flattened me and then stood to take on the threat.

"Dragon is here now," Hewitt said peacefully.

"Hewitt!" I scrambled up and instead of racing to make sure Hewitt was okay, nearly ran into a malevolent purple eyeball peering around Derrick. "Lindis!" I forgot myself and threw my arms around her skinny, scaled neck. "You're safe! You're alive, you're *dragon!*" She didn't really have shoulders to grab, so I patted the hump that turned into a wing. "Lindis?"

Derrick gently moved me aside. "Lindis?" he repeated.

Purple scales curled in on themselves as the dragon listed to the side like a pony about to fall over. Her eyes closed and only a tree near her behind kept her upright.

"Lindis! Are you hurt?" I scooted out from behind Derrick to reach her.

Her eyes slit open, but she didn't try to straighten. I ran my hand across her back. "I don't see any blood."

Derrick, without moving, used his nose to confirm my finding. "I'm going after her parents."

"Hewitt—oh bother." How could a four-year-old guard a dragon while I went for food?

Hewitt came over and sat by Lindis' tail. He patted it. "We go soon."

He was crazy. I ran to the cellar, knowing there was plenty of dried deer meat there. Of course, it was possible food wouldn't help her at all, but what else could I offer?

By the time I returned, Lindis had recovered enough to drink half the stream and leave muddy swirls. She leaned drunkenly over the water, one wing out to keep her from falling in.

I left the food, went back for more and from inside the house, grabbed my scratchy school tunic in case she wanted to change.

Panting, I arrived with the next load to find she had finished the meat. Her head was now human, but the rest of her stayed dragon. Her tail, instead of ending in a sharp spike, was smoothed to a rounded stump—most likely because she had become aware enough to realize Hewitt had decided to plant himself next to her tail.

"What happened?" I asked, handing her more food.

She chewed eagerly. "Did you pull down the cage?"

It took a lot more chewing and explanation before I was able to confirm that I probably had. "But then what happened?"

Lindis smiled. "I recovered the ring. But I'm not sure it matters. I was already able to change almost all the way back. The ring contained the gryphon's blood and mine, and he was dead. After I..." she paused long enough for a concerned glance at Hewitt, who had taken her tail and curled it around himself. "I dispensed some justice. But before I did, I learned a glyph for showing other glyphs." She drew a symbol in the dirt. "It showed me some interesting spells around the camp, including a pentagram set up that was the transport spell. I think he used it to get into the dragon ballroom, but I wasn't sure of the symbol for the ballroom. I only knew it was a transport spell because it was very similar to the one your cousin Lonnie used when he grabbed me."

She drew a symbol next to the other one in the sand, but it wasn't one I recognized. "I wanted to get back here quickly, but wasn't taking any chances. If I ended back inside the dragon lair, the dragon council would quarantine me and probably hold me prisoner for my own protection."

"Most likely." I provided a quick rundown on the gryphons who were being held and some of the arguments I'd heard.

"That's dragon politics, all right. I didn't have time to recharge the crystal you gave me so I used you and your tie to it as the focus in the pentagram hoping it would bring me directly to you. Without much energy in the crystal, I had to use my own energy for the actual transport spell, but it didn't work very well. "

I swallowed. "You tried something that demanding—" I shook my head. "You're lucky you didn't—"

"No wonder you call your cousin an idiot. I was certain I'd managed to behead myself on the way through. Everything went completely black. I tried to hold a glide, but it was like tumbling straight through the air into rocks. I won't be trying that again anytime soon."

I nodded my agreement, hard. "You weren't looking very good when you landed."

The sharp bellow of a dragon call disrupted us.

Lindis' parents flew once overhead as a warning of their arrival, and then made gentle landings in the glen. They changed quickly, although scales served as clothing. The silver tips of Jared's scales glinted in the sunlight. Lindis' mother, Roelle, moved even faster than her husband; a lethal maroon streak rushing through the shadows of the trees.

"Lindis!" Roelle fussed, hugged and inspected every possible inch while Jared kept one eye on his surroundings in case of danger.

When Roelle finally calmed down, Jared asked, "The ring?"

Lindis held it up. "When the gryphon died, most of the magic went with him. The rest dissipated when I killed Camden-WhoCouldn'tWaitToDie."

"What if someone reactivates it?" her mother worried.

"Camden didn't know the whole spell." Lindis explained how he had tried to see the glyphs. "The gryphon kept part of it hidden from him. The only person who knew the entire spell was the gryphon, and he's dead."

Derrick, who once again appeared so quietly I didn't hear him approach, said, "If any of the students at Gorgon University played a part in the spelling of that ring, most of them are also dead. The school burned."

"What about a book like that one?" Lindis asked, pointing to the spell book still on the ground where we had been working. "He must have kept notes."

Hewitt stood. "The gryphon cave!" He repeated the gesture from before, raising his fist into the air. "We go to mama."

Jared blinked ebony eyes. His hair was as close to midnight as his daughter's, but it was tipped with silver on the ends, just as his scales were. "Now is not a good time to try a visit to the gryphon's territory. We're at a stalemate waiting until the gryphon clan comes up with an explanation for how and why one of their own hired a mage to trap a dragon."

Lindis snorted. "Better also ask them how Gryphon Alcen broke the geas to use magic. Of the two, he was more powerful than Camden, although Camden started out as the teacher from what he said."

"Do the gryphons see well at night?" I asked.

Lindis flicked her purple gaze my way. "They use their eagle vision in the daytime, but they are also part lion. They don't have a problem with night vision."

"So the warmest part of the day would be better?" I watched Hewitt as I asked the question. He nodded eagerly.

Jared shook his head. "They are neither night nor day creatures, but a mix. They have sentries and ground patrols, just as we do. It's doubtful we can get in without being seen, and fighting our way back out would be impossible unless we took an entire contingent of dragons. That would be a full war effort, and nothing that we could pull off quickly."

"But Lindis knows the transport spell," I said slowly. "And I know most of it. What we really need is crystals. Several of them, powered up and ready to use." The white was already ready to go. "Anyone know where we can get some?"

Lindis' lips curled into a smile for the first time since her escape. "Ah, little mage. Yes, crystals we have."

And we had people who knew how to use them to store energy. "I've seen the transportation spell a few times now, but I need to learn it thoroughly. Can you teach me the symbols you used?"

Lindis tapped her head. "Perfect recall. It's only a matter of me understanding what I'm looking at. But we'll need something as the focus. I had to change the focus of the one Camden had to you and your crystal. What can we use to get to the gryphon lair?"

I turned to the seer. "Hewitt? Can you draw a symbol that will take us to your mother?" He didn't answer me, but there was no stronger tie in life than a child's tie to his mother. Surely there was a way to make it work. Risky, yes. But it had to work, right? "We need to set things up so that we can transport back here quickly."

Jared nodded. "I'll get the crystals." Before leaving, he touched a hand to his daughter's face. He was a very large man, but the gesture was as gentle as a breeze.

She responded by touching his arm with her wing.

I ignored the display, too busy hoping we could figure out a way in and back out. More than that, I wished we had some idea of how much power was required, because in my experience, there was never enough power to cover the unexpected.

Chapter 19

We worked hard on our first plan, but Hewitt couldn't or wouldn't provide enough information to magic us in. He either didn't know a glyph that would work or had other seer reasons for not telling. Appearing out of thin air in a gryphon's lair with no warning and no preparation wasn't necessarily a wise choice, so it could easily be that Hewitt sensed disaster.

While the crystals provided by the dragons charged, we mapped out a strategy. "Who might be in the gryphon's den besides Hewitt's mother?" I wondered.

Lindis had no idea, and her parents could only speculate. "Alcen wasn't a young gryphon, but when he mated, it didn't last long, not even by human standards. It's possible he chose Hewitt's mother as a new mate, but gryphons are notoriously anti-social outside their prides. They live in rock outcroppings and mountainsides that are nearly impossible to reach without wings. A human would be at a distinct disadvantage," Roelle said.

"Do the gryphons want more territory?" I asked. "Is that why they might want a dragon under their control?"

There was an uncomfortable silence before Derrick said, "Most clans, prides, and packs would consider an alliance with the dragons a good thing."

"And a gryphon with magic...and control of a dragon. That could cause disastrous problems for human territories."

Everyone glared at me when I said it. "What? Alcen was headmaster at Gorgon for years. He wasn't learning magic so he could sit in his den and bake pies! Lindis told us Camden wanted Anton. Alcen either wanted to rule there too or at least planned it as a first stop."

Roelle sighed, stressed enough that steam billowed around her. "There's been arguments for a long time about how much interaction we should have with the human territories. There are those who wish to conquer it and those who wish to ignore it. After the last war, none of us wanted anything to do with humans, but that might have been part of the geas. The wall between us has been coming down in the last two centuries, and it's quite possible Alcen wanted to be the first to grab territory."

"Are the gryphons as long-lived as the dragons?"

Lindis nodded. "Gryphon Alcen was older than my mother. He could very well have known how and why the veil was there if he teased it out of his memory. He was definitely alive when it came down."

Before I could ask more questions, a large hawk, mostly white, landed in a nearby tree. It wasn't Shae; it was smaller and less brown. Like Shae, he changed to human on his way from a half leap out of the tree. His hair was a very light blonde, thin and silky.

"Shae's son, Falk," Derrick whispered near my ear.

Shae's eyes were reddish brown, but Falk's were yellow. Instead of pants, his legs remained covered in stunted feathers that looked almost like down. "The wolves and hawks have met at the noon roost," he said. "News came during the talks that you had dragons gathered here, and I was sent to see what was happening. Father assumed it was either Lindis or a rescue attempt by your mage." He turned his yellow gaze my way. "I'm Falk until I earn another name. Father says as a goodwill gesture he will see that your message is delivered to your parents. In the meantime, he asks for a return favor."

I was no more happy than a noble to be caught on the wrong end of a favor. "He cannot wish to be involved in rescuing Lindis. We already did that."

Falk smiled. When he did, his whole face changed from craggy angles to a softer boyish grin. "No, he wishes to know who claims you and your hatchling, because after due thought, he believes you might be worth fighting for if it happens to be a human from Birk who has abandoned you both."

I refused to look at Derrick. He had warned me against trying to thwart the rules here.

Before I could devise a clever answer, Derrick interceded. "It hardly matters, Falk. She has said she is claimed."

Falk took a deep breath, expanding his naked chest as though fluffing invisible feathers in warning. Unlike his father, he wasn't preening and showing off, but as handsome and muscular as he was, he had no need anyway. "Father indicated it might be worth my while to know. I trust his judgment." Flirtatiously, his eyes traveled the length of my person. "I can say at first glance, he is probably right, although I do believe his interest was piqued because she is a mage, while mine might be more personal."

I didn't appreciate being assessed like a calf at market. "We can discuss this huge favor your father needs, but not until we are free and clear of the threat from the gryphon. Once Lindis is safe, no one will be interested in me because, you see, I am not a mage yet. If your father is after such, he'll do better to hire one who at least managed to graduate." I did need a job so it seemed prudent to leave the door open. "If he has a few years and patience, maybe he can hire me after I have finished school."

Falk showed no reaction. His gaze was on Derrick, who stared coldly back.

"And just how do you intend to protect Lindis from a dead gryphon?" Falk kept his attention on Derrick when he asked the question.

Lindis answered. "Alcen is the one who spelled the ring. He's dead, but if he wrote the means to that end, any such spell belongs to me."

I nodded. "We've a gryphon lair to raid and no time to worry about claims on someone like who does not matter in the least." I turned to collect the crystals from the sunlight. We had all memorized the transport spell along with the one to reveal glyphs. In case Hewitt's mother was in a magical cage, I knew the drain spell and had showed it to the dragons. If something happened to me, they would not forget the glyphs.

My statement or movement finally diverted Falk's attention. "You're planning to approach a gryphon lair?"

"Gryphon Alcen's lair to be exact," Lindis said.

Falk uncrossed his arms. "And if you recover this information you seek, the dragons would then be the keepers of this spell. We didn't know of this at the meeting."

"The notes may not even exist," I pointed out. "And if they do, they might not be complete or the spell might not be repeatable."

"Perhaps Father would rather change the favor to obtaining a copy of any notes."

"Perhaps you should focus on what you can do to be of help in exchange for any favors," Derrick growled.

Falk didn't hesitate. "I do know the location of Gryphon Alcen's lair."

"I'm already certain of it myself," Jared countered.

Falk scratched his chin. "We are aligned favorably with the gryphons. It wouldn't be unusual for me to request a meeting with them, especially given the current state of affairs. I can keep a sentry or two busy with my request." He shook his head. "But even a meeting would not stop them from watching their territory carefully. You'll have to fly in high. And dive fast."

Jared gave an impatient puff and beckoned him over. "We've no quarrel with you. If you wish to help, we may as well use it. We know the locations of the den and the main sentry points. Let's see if what I know matches what you know."

While Falk and Jared compared notes and flight plans, I repacked my pack. Lindis strung some of the charged crystals on a leather band.

My clothing had pockets for several crystals, but Derrick took a leather necklace from Lindis and looped it and its dark purple crystal around my neck. He left his hand on my shoulder longer than necessary. When I turned to thank him, Falk was watching.

"I hope you'll remember my help favorably, my lady," Falk said.

"I hope we all make it out alive to tell the tales," I replied before remembering my courtly manners. Belatedly, I dipped my head respectfully. "Any help you bring to bear on our survival is greatly appreciated and will be remembered."

Derrick tightened his grip on my shoulder. He made no noise, but I felt a warning rumble in his chest.

Falk switched his gaze from me to him. "I'll do reconnaissance and see if I can't work up an additional distraction. I've friends who will view it as an amusing afternoon lark." With a bow in my direction, he took to the sky in a powerful leap just as his father had done.

I took a deep breath. "We'd better get those notes before every creature from here to Central goes after them."

Lindis reached a wing in my direction. "To me then, little mage." She flipped me up, pack and all, before I could protest.

"Hewitt, hurry!" I leaned to him, but Lindis' mother lifted him up instead.

"You are with my hatchling. I'll take yours." She smiled serenely and for a moment I thought perhaps she had missed part of the conversation. But she was dragon. We had talked of Hewitt's mother. She knew.

Derrick was heaviest so it made sense he go with Lindis' father. He awaited Jared's permission before leaping aboard as gracefully as though he were part bird—or part dragon.

As dragon wings beat the air, Hewitt lifted his fist and laughed gleefully, flying at last.

Chapter 20

The dragons flew high enough that the frigid air crawled inside my skin and left me gasping. The gryphons weren't as capable as the dragons at these higher altitudes, but neither was this furless, scaleless human. Knowing we didn't have far to go helped, but when we began the dive, my stomach flipped over so hard it could have killed me before the cold had a chance.

There wasn't time to note much more than a rocky outcrop nearing at an alarming rate. In a band beneath it there was greenery; trees, more rocks, hills and a mountain off to one side. From the discussions, Gryphon Alcen had lived in a den between Three Sisters Peaks. Since there were three peaks, there was some question as to whether we'd be able to land on the right ridge, but between Falk and Jared's input, the dragons were confident.

None of the discussions meant anything to me. I had paid enough attention to note that if I was grounded for some reason, east was the direction of safety—past another set of mountains that was full of gryphons. Within the next twenty miles or so, there was a short territory of were-panthers and one ruled by bears.

Lindis banked hard, leaving my brain somewhere behind us.

It took me several seconds to realize that two of the boulders below were gryphons guarding an entrance. "Uh-oh."

One of the sentries launched to meet us. His claws were tucked rather than extended to attack, but that was probably because the dragon was above him. If we tried to land, the gryphon would be above us and able to score some damage.

The second gryphon left its post, flying low and away. Jared, with Derrick on his back, veered off to give chase. My stomach found me again, but clenched with fear, it wasn't an improvement.

We hadn't talked about becoming separated. The plan had been to drop Derrick near the entrance. He'd do quick reconnaissance with Jared as backup before the rest of us landed.

With one guard rising to meet us and the other racing for reinforcements, Jared had made the logical decision to follow the gryphon headed for backup. If we were lucky, he'd stop the gryphon from warning the others.

As if they had practiced it their whole lives, Lindis' mother engaged the gryphon on our tail with a burst of fire. Lindis snapped her neck around and belched her own flame. The swirling vortex nearly set my hair on fire.

"I guess we're not pretending to be stopping by for tea."

The gryphon dodged both blasts with a quick dive.

Lindis neared the cave entrance and dipped. "Be quick," she shouted. "I'll land on the next pass as soon as I check on Mother."

I fell more than jumped, dropping to the boulder where the first gryphon had been stationed. It would have been harder to stay balanced there than roll down the side where it was safer for me.

"We're bringing Hewitt," I yelled into the cavern on my right. Hopefully Hewitt's mother was alive. If she was being held captive, maybe she'd convince her captors to let us bring her child to her.

I clutched the purple crystal nestled between my breasts and completed the glyph for a transport spell that would take me back to the pentagram at Derrick's house. If a gryphon came out of the cavern or dropped down on me from above, I would have no choice but to say the word of power and get myself gone.

Once I had an exit plan, I peeked from around the boulder. Wind whipped a few loose strands of hair across my face. The air carried the chill of ice and snow from yonder, higher peaks. The sky was empty of dragons and gryphons.

A tiny speck in the distance could be either or neither.

I stepped inside the opening quickly, both to get out of sight and to get it over with.

Darkness cloaked me in its welcoming embrace. I smelled nothing but rock and dirt. Without the chill wind, there was a sense of respite.

The plan had been for at least two of us, possibly all of us, to enter together. We hadn't discussed only one of us making it, and it would be foolhardy for me to go alone. I was the least prepared to fight a gryphon or anyone else.

I edged back to the opening and checked for backup. Before I could talk myself forward or back, a hawk spiraled past, missing my head by inches. Wings snapped out to break his fall, but the bird slammed into the darkness with an alarming crunch.

"Falk?" I slid back into the yawning gloom.

"The gryphons are on their way," he half squawked, half breathed.

I drew a glyph and muttered a word to light the purple crystal just enough to see.

Falk was sprawled against the cave wall. Shadows and boulders surrounded him. One arm hadn't changed when he went human. The wing remained at an odd angle.

"Falk! Are you crazed?"

"Apparently." He winced. "What did I hit? There was nothing there."

"Are you hurt badly?" I set a small brownish-white crystal near the entrance where it wouldn't be noticed. The right word would blow any attack backwards, at least temporarily. Since gryphons were large, it wasn't likely we'd miss one skulking towards us.

I hurried over to Falk's side. "Can you fix your wing?" Since nothing had appeared to kill us from within, I brightened the lantern spell. It was a new experience having plenty of charged crystals to work with.

In the purple-blue light, Falk still looked dazed, and he hadn't stopped panting. "It's...okay." Slowly, the wing morphed to a human arm, but he continued to hold it away from his body. Sweat dripped down his brow, and his face was white with pain. "I won't be flying out with it."

"The dragons can get you out," I said. "Or I will."

"How?" His eyes rolled back and forth nervously.

I didn't bother to answer him. Instead I called out, "Hello? We've brought Hewitt." There was no echo. Nothing but darkness loomed outside the small pool of light.

I slid my foot forward slowly. The only sounds were that of my heartbeat and Falk's pained breathing.

It was only two shaky steps forward when my boot hit a solid barrier. There was a spark of light at my foot, but otherwise the cave remained the kin of midnight. I felt along the invisible surface with my hands. My hasty lantern light did nothing to illuminate beyond the barrier. Falk must have hit the invisible blockage when he tried to land.

I pulled power from the crystal at my neck and drew the reveal glyph that Lindis had taught me.

Sure enough, symbols lit up the cavern, throwing bands of light and shadows—but only in our direction. Everything behind the ward was still black.

"Hewitt?" a voice called out softly. "Are you there?"

My heart nearly stopped before beating furiously. "He's with the dragons," I answered. "They'll land in a minute. Are you—Mistress Alcen?"

"Yes. It is I—Teal. Do you really have Hewitt?"

I certainly hoped so, although I couldn't put my hands on him right this second. "Is it safe for me to dismantle this ward and come further in?"

There was a long pause. Finally, in a firm voice, she demanded, "What happened to Alcen?"

Tricky. If she cared about him and viewed me as the bearer of bad news...The dragons had best have our backs. I felt more than a little trapped against this ward, and I didn't recognize any of the symbols...no wait! At least one was a dragon and there was a form that was almost exactly the same shape as the ring that bound Lindis.

"What happened to Alcen?" Teal demanded again.

"He's dead," I said. There was no sugar-coating it. "Did he leave you caged?"

Teal gave a choked laugh, but the miserable sound cut off almost instantly. "Why would he need a cage? How would I escape? I can't fly!"

"But how did Hewitt get away?" Ah, there were more symbols than I expected, but several were the same ones cousin Lonnie had used when he caged Lindis.

A long-suffering sigh had no trouble making it across the barrier. "Hewitt disappeared before the gryphon brought me up here. He does it all the time. The gryphon devises spell after spell to keep him with us, but it never works for long. Do you have my son?"

"He's with the dragons. They haven't landed yet." I pulled from the purple again, using a bit of energy to rub out the symbols I recognized. It was dangerous and more than a bit foolhardy. If I guessed wrong, the magic could release the energy all at once and smack into me with a blast that would send me halfway down the mountain.

The dragon was an unnecessary symbol. There was no need to protect against them here, and if they were caged behind this ward, well then, it was time to let them out. I wasn't sure about the gryphon...but I erased it as well.

Unexpectedly, the wall snapped down, causing me to stumble back a step.

With it gone, light shone from within the cavern. I edged forward, dagger in one hand and the blue ready to shove away anything that got too close. "Stay back," I warned Falk in a whisper.

He ignored me, stepping up to my side.

Before I advanced more than a step, noise from the entrance had me turning back, dagger raised and a word at the ready. The crystal I had left at the opening was a one-shot deal, but it would at least give me time.

To my immense relief Derrick rolled to his feet just inside the glow from my purple necklace.

"Haven't you the sense to wait?" he growled.

"*Where is my son?*"

I flipped back around. Someone had brightened the lanterns, dispelling any notion of a simple cave and illuminating housing that was every bit as plush as the castle at Birk. Clever tapestries on the walls were lit from behind such that two of them pretended to be windows. Small tunnels in the ceiling were either fitted with crystals or they pulled in sunlight directly.

Bookcases lined one entire wall and continued partway down a long hallway. The palace would be jealous of the fine wool rugs and a set of table and chairs decorated with gilded lion's feet.

The first person I saw was not Teal, but I recognized the dark braided woman all the same. She hunkered down along one side of the bookcase. "Brittany?" My mouth gaped, but then I gasped, *"And Irwin? I thought you escaped!"*

Brittany had her slingshot out, but made no move to use it. "We were captured on our way past Gorgon. I made the mistake of trusting Mage-Master Alcen and we ended up trapped instead."

"He still intended to force Irwin to marry the dragon?" I asked with disbelief.

Teal said softly, "I think not. We had all become quite expendable." She was perched up on a high ledge that might have held books or other utensils at one time. It was inaccessible enough that a sword couldn't reach her easily. Something in her hand glinted. It wasn't a crystal and was too short to be a dagger, but if she threw it at us, it would probably do significant damage. "Master Alcen wanted the dragon for his own if he had another chance at it."

Brittany sniped, "If you'd kept yourself out of trouble, I wouldn't have been dragged to Gorgon and gotten in this mess at all! You were supposed to guard the prince, not get pregnant with a useless child."

Teal's head dipped slightly but she kept her eyes on us, unable or unwilling to meet Brittany's accusation.

"Are you referring to the useless child who has saved your hide twice now?" I kept my voice even with effort. "That child would be Hewitt, the one who helped you rescue Prince Irwin back at the church. And it was Hewitt who brought us here to rescue you now." I met Brittany's eyes without flinching. "Seems to me you ought to thank fate for looking kindly on you."

Irwin nodded. "Too true." He rested patiently against the smooth rock wall near Brittany. His arm looked as though it had healed, but he carried no weapon.

"Where is Hewitt?" Teal demanded again.

I glanced at Derrick. He said, "Soon. He's lighter than we are. Roelle is not having any trouble carrying him and keeping up her end of the battle, but they're going to have to land and make this a last stand soon." He pulled out the largest crystal he carried. "There are more people here to transport than we anticipated. Maybe some of them should have minded their own business."

I rolled my eyes. "Falk can't fly out. He's coming with us."

"I'm not leaving without Hewitt," Teal shouted.

"Don't worry, neither are we," I assured her. Derrick approached Brittany and Irwin cautiously.

"You need not fear us," Brittany said. "We're completely trapped behind a ward. My sister is too much of a coward to release the spell the gryphon left."

I sputtered. "Sister? But...*What?!?*"

Derrick ignored us and began drawing the symbols we'd need to leave, marking them with chalk in case he was interrupted. Using chalk meant any of us could see where he left off and continue the pattern.

I helped Derrick, drawing from the last symbol backwards, while he worked forward. Since no information seemed forthcoming, I asked, "You and Brittany are sisters?"

Teal nodded, but Brittany just raised her chin. Teal dropped her eyes and clarified, "Not any longer. I was disowned once I became pregnant. Brittany and I belong to a long line of warriors trained to guard the royal family of Anton. I was sent to Gorgon two years before Irwin as security detail. The king had decided that he wanted his second born—Irwin—to become the castle wizard."

I blinked. "But Hewitt said the gryphon isn't his father. How did you end up with him?"

"Traitor!" Brittany yelled.

"What was I to do?" Teal retorted. "Let my son starve after I was abandoned? Once I was pregnant, not only did Hewitt's father not want me, neither did my family. I remained at Gorgon as a maid. Gryphon Alcen took pity on me. He wanted a wife with a legitimate pedigree into Anton, plus I could help him test spells. He didn't care that he wasn't Hewitt's father."

My brain raced around in circles much faster than the transport pentagram I was forgetting to work on. "Did you know he was a gryphon? From Wendal?"

Teal hopped down from her shelf. "It's a long story, and I'm not certain I've all of it correct. It started too long ago when Gorgon was first established. I believe you met Camden in a scuffle over Irwin?"

I nodded. "Unfortunately."

"Camden's great-uncle was Gorgon, the founder of the university. He came to Birk and opened Gorgon University because he was intrigued by Wendal. Gorgon designed the reveal glyph that you just used on my ward at the entrance. He wanted to use the glyph to study why no one could get closer to Wendal. Of course, once he could see the glyphs, in his youthful and foolish enthusiasm, he erased some of the symbols so that he could get across."

"And the veil began to dissolve!"

She nodded. "Gorgon apparently had no idea how to bring it back up again. He knew what the glyphs looked like, but hadn't the power to recreate the veil. He founded the school to work on the problem, but if he ever discovered how to do it, he took the secret with him to his grave."

I had stopped even pretending to draw the necessary symbols, because I had to know. "How did the gryphon get involved with the school and when?"

"I'm not certain." She shrugged, a tired gesture with only one shoulder. "Alcen was already in charge by the time I arrived. He was deep in his research, trying to discover everything Gorgon knew about the veil. Gorgon was long dead, although he had devised spells that allowed him to live well past a hundred.

She paced close enough to watch what we were doing, forcing my focus back to drawing the glyphs. The weapon in her hand was more obvious now; a metal hilt with no blade. The metal glowed with the power it contained.

She pocketed it quickly but kept her hand on it as she continued her story. "Gorgon wasn't making much progress until Camden showed up ahead of Prince Irwin's entourage. Camden grew up at Gorgon because he was Gorgon's great-nephew. The one thing Camden did in his youth was talk his dying great-uncle into teaching him the reveal spell. Camden was certain that the spell was all he'd need to become the next wizard of Anton. He was wrong, of course. Anton's king wanted his second son to become the wizard.

"Camden spent time at Gorgon off and on complaining about

having his heritage stolen by the prince. Gryphon Alcen finally found out about the reveal spell and convinced Camden to teach it to him in exchange for a promise that Camden would have the mage spot in Anton once Prince Irwin was installed on the throne."

"But the firstborn is in line for the throne, and the king is still alive!"

"Details." She shrugged. "Once Alcen had the glyph, he could see things Gorgon had hidden and hidden well. Alcen kept Camden around because he believed Camden might know other important glyphs. At first Alcen schemed to have Irwin marry the dragon, but later," she sighed. "I think he only kept Irwin and the rest of us as leverage."

"You may as well release Brittany and Irwin," I told her. "We've got to get out of here."

"Where is my—"

Roelle glided in so fast, there was a rush of displaced air. Her wings were tucked tight to make it into the gryphon den, right until the last possible second. Lindis landed behind her and was half changed in an instant. She carried Hewitt. "Draw the glyphs," she shouted. "Go!"

She belched fire behind her, and as her mother turned around, she echoed the flames alongside her daughter.

Jared flew right through the flames as if they weren't there. He landed awkwardly on one foot and didn't bother to change to human. Blood poured from his back and dripped down one side.

"Drop the ward," I urged Teal.

She ignored me in favor of hugging Hewitt. Tears rolled down her face. Her face had aged since I'd seen her last, but it still did not match her snow-white hair.

Hewitt tugged at her hand. "We go."

With a flick of Teal's wrist, Brittany and Irwin were free. They ran to Derrick.

Derrick said, "We had better go in small groups. This diagram isn't big enough for all of us. Jared, you go first."

With Falk, there were four people in the ring already. Add a dragon...oh Lord, that was a lot to transport, and the dragon was injured.

"I can hold them off!" Jared protested. "Roelle, go!" he commanded his wife.

I grabbed Teal's shoulders. "Do you know the transport spell? Why haven't you used it?"

"Where would I go? And never without Hewitt. I'm not sure it will work on him."

"What?!?"

"I've tried to find him that way before, by transporting myself to him. It doesn't work. And I can't call him back to me either."

Derrick caught my worried gaze with a flare of his wolf eyes. He stepped outside the circle. There was a loud rumbling from what had been the front entrance. Boulders tumbled from above and careened past the front.

"They'll bury us?" I gasped in dismay. "Teal! Where are the gryphon's notes?"

She shook her head. "There aren't any."

"Impossible!" I didn't believe her. Lindis' parents shot more fire out the entrance, warning away a gryphon who checked on us a little too closely.

Lindis, her hand on the rock wall, said, "The stones tell me that there is another exit, but these aren't dragon stones from our lair. They sing to the tune of the dwarf king, and the dwarves are obviously taking the side of the gryphons!"

"Hewitt needs to go first," I said. "If he can't be transported—" One of us would have to stay and try to make it out the other exit. Of course the dwarves would probably close that exit too, but there wasn't time to worry about it now. "Teal. The notes," I begged softly. "Whatever we can grab and take with us."

"They're better buried!"

"Probably so, but don't think this mountain will stay that way if even a single person believes we left anything here. If dwarves can bury us, they can unbury the notes and books later."

A boulder cracked free from the ceiling, taking out the lights recessed in the small tunnels. The crystal lanterns on the wall remained, but the room dimmed ominously.

Roelle grabbed Hewitt, shoved Falk into the circle and then planted herself in front of her husband. "Go with them." One command. Eons of meaning. Years of history.

"No." His black eyes snapped with determination.

"You have a better chance of convincing the council to send help."

I stopped wasting time. The gryphon had shelves of leather bound books. Some looked like spell texts. The best way to tell was to use the reveal glyph, but there wasn't time. I couldn't transport them all...then again, there were no rules about a circle. Connected to the ceiling and stretched to the other diagram...

I began drawing, branching from one end of the completed pentagram, creating a larger second one that would encircle the bookcases. If no one wanted to be the first to leave, fine. We'd all die together or go together.

Derrick was the first to realize I was linking two pentagrams together. He grinned. "Why not?" He knelt at the opposite end and worked the chalk quickly.

We'd take as much as we could possibly carry. Linked together maybe there would be enough energy.

A low rumble interrupted my concentration just before Teal screamed, "Hewitt!"

Dust showered down on us from the ceiling. "How are they moving the rock?" I yelled.

"Who cares?" Brittany shouted. "Someone send us!"

There was no reason she and the others inside the pentagram couldn't go. Derrick had already completed it. I stepped over and placed a crystal inside the pentagram. Falk immediately stepped out of it. "I can carry some of the books from the hallway."

His eyes held fear, but courage too. "Grab some then," I said. "I can't tell you which, if any, will do the most good."

Teal nearly bowled me over when she clutched at my shoulders. "Where is he? *Where is Hewitt??*"

My legs settled into a crouch to keep from falling. "He was right next to you, holding your skirts!"

A chunk of the ceiling crashed next to Lindis where she had taken over drawing for me.

"Hewitt?" I yelled, but the rumbling drowned me out. "Hewitt!"

"The bedroom." Teal spun away at a run. "Either that or he went for the tunnel. He doesn't like magic."

I chased after her. Brittany screamed about activating the circle and her job of saving Irwin for Anton. As I followed Teal, I heard the prince say, "Maybe it's time to stop running."

We found Hewitt in a side room behind a long tapestry. It was a bedroom all right and an opulent one at that. The bed was large enough for a human or gryphon. It contained enough silk pillows to form a giant nest.

Hewitt pointed at the wall near the bed. There was nothing there but carved granite, much like the rest of the walls.

"Oh, Hewitt," his mother whispered.

I sat next to him, cross-legged, ignoring the enraged mountain still dumping debris. A large crack appeared in the floor, snaking out from under the nest of pillows.

"He's hidden it, has he?" I drew the reveal glyph, but nothing happened.

Hewitt leaned his head against my arm. The side of his face was smeared with dirt and the track of a tear. He was very tired. And probably hungry. It had been a rather long day for a four year old. He reached out and touched the granite again, but his mother scooped him up from behind.

Lindis ran in, shouting, "The back escape corridor has collapsed. Little mage, we've got to go. Now!"

I shut her out and closed my eyes, feeling the stone in front of me. It wasn't just illusion, there was a barrier. But if it was the same spell as the other barriers, why didn't the glyphs show up? I couldn't see what I was erasing, but I tried it anyway. "Hewitt, can you show me the border?"

Teal shook her head and spun for the main room. Hewitt pillowed his head on her shoulder. His sad eyes found mine, but then he was gone behind the tapestry.

"Zoe, now!" Lindis commanded.

"Give me the ring," I said, my hand out.

"What?"

"*Hurry up, dammit.*"

Lindis pulled the ring from her finger and gave it to me. I drew faster than I ever had in my life, repeating the "Y" that formed a gutter to a drain. I used the ring, the ring spelled by Alcen, and one that contained his blood. The ring was the focus and one of my crystals powered the spell.

The first word of power I uttered was lost beneath a roar of an avalanche above our heads. The gryphons and dwarves were shaking loose the entire mountain. I felt the power leak from the crystal, but the Y didn't snap like it should have.

Derrick yelled, "Zoe!" He was suddenly there, behind me. He leaned to pick me up, but before he could throw me over his shoulder, I pushed out my arm.

"No, not yet! I'll blast you backwards, I will!" It was an empty threat, but he hesitated long enough for me to turn back to the granite. "One second. I've got it." I knew what it had to be. It was magic like Lindis used, magic inside of magic, like when she reached into the fire. I redrew the last line connecting to the sapphire and said the word again, using the sapphire as the power source instead of my crystal.

The granite wall dissolved. I reached in and snagged the bundled packet within.

Derrick hoisted me from my waist and carried me backwards. I barely had time to scoop up Lindis' ring before he hauled me away.

The walls tumbled around us as he ran.

Chapter 21

Derrick didn't release me even after we stumbled into the pentagram in the outer room. The first pentagram he had drawn lit up like a beacon, flashing briefly before Teal and her son Hewitt disappeared. I didn't blame her one bit. If she took her hands off Hewitt, no telling where he might go next. Thank all that was, when she tried the transport spell, Hewitt transported just fine.

Three dragons, a wolf, and me stretched across the linked pentagrams. Lindis' parents were in the first pentagram with Falk. Irwin and Brittany reached across to us in the second. The three not doing magic had loaded texts into the circle and across their backs. There was no way to know whether the inanimate objects we weren't holding would come with us. I had my bundle from the bedroom and touched only Derrick as he wasn't inclined to set me down.

"Now!" Lindis shouted.

Derrick's word and mine were the same. To my surprise, Lindis and her parents echoed it as well. Dragons and their superior hearing. Did all of Wendal now know it?

In our desperation to escape, we may have used too much magic. Or maybe the rumbling of the earth followed us just long enough to cause havoc.

The gut-wrenching transport included at least two large boulders that were on the way down. Dust followed us as though determined to suffocate us. The first thing my coughing lungs allowed me to see was the bookcase, tipped over on top of Brittany. The books must have knocked her out solidly because she lay unmoving.

Hewitt, free from his mother again, was sprawled on his little butt. A flying book had mashed open against his chest. A loose page from another dangled from his hair. Three more texts were behind him, flung into the bushes and trees. There was movement underneath a tapestry.

The table with the lion's feet had come through, but the couch had not. I hadn't seen where the final glyphs for the second pentagram were drawn. It hardly mattered. One chair had transported with us, but it had shattered from the landing or been smashed by the stones that had fallen just as we activated the spell.

Hewitt's mother struggled out from under the heavy tapestry and limped to her wayward child. That would teach her to stand around lollygagging after transporting ahead of everyone else. Next time maybe she'd move out of the way and take shelter.

Derrick's parents, Seth and Anne, rushed around the side of a large oak and then stopped to gape. Star ran into them from behind. Her hand lost the grip she had on a very subdued Lonnie.

Seth said, "We brought your cousin. We thought he might be of some assistance if something went wrong."

Sad when the best wizard you had was Lonnie.

I spit dirt and rubbed at my face. "What say you, cousin Lonnie? Have you a solution?"

The one thing Lonnie was good at was appearances. The moment he realized attention was on him, he straightened, threw his shoulders back and gave a wizardly sniff, one he had practiced for hours in front of a mirror. "Looks as though you could use a bath, cousin."

Master of the obvious.

Falk stumbled to a nearby tree and lost the contents of his stomach.

"Needs a splint for his arm," Derrick said.

Derrick's mother asked, "Can he change back and forth first? It will help it to align properly." Even as she asked, she tore the bottom of her shirt into a strip.

I tossed the gryphon ring to Lindis. From the look on her face, she had forgotten it. Her fist snatched it out of the air. She stared down at it, but instead of putting it on her finger, she dangled it in front of her face for a long moment before dropping it in her mouth. She swallowed silently.

At my look of astonishment, she nodded. "The magic was gone from it in any case, and with no one left alive who knows how to make it, melted metal is the best place for it to be." She patted her stomach. "If anyone were to figure out how to see the glyphs on it, they could potentially recreate such a ring. But not if it is melted."

"What about the sapphire?"

She shrugged. "Gems are never a problem for a dragon. That is the one thing that has troubled me all along about the ring, especially after you told me that blood was used. When Camden revealed some of the glyphs, I could see the blood inside the gem. I felt it. It was mine."

I thought long and hard. There was really only one answer. "Only a dragon could embed blood in a gem?"

"That was my first thought. After witnessing how much the dwarves are helping the gryphons...it's possible they know the technique. But either way, there is a traitor in our midst. Whoever it is doesn't need to know that I suspect duplicity." A puff of smoke escaped one side of her mouth. "Yet."

I shivered. "Woe be to him when you find him."

"Woe indeed," she promised, clenching her fist tight.

Tired though I was, I proceeded to undo the glyphs and crystals that had served to guide us home.   Not that the gryphons could possibly follow us through since the dwarves had buried the place in stone. Cleaning it up was simply a good mage standard.

We spent the next two hours erasing glyphs, eating, and getting Falk to his roost. Lindis had to fly him because Roelle was busy taking care of her husband. Jared's wound was deep, and healing it was going to require gut-wrenching changing back and forth to speed the process. It would be a good idea if someone in Wendal studied the arts of healing magic. Too bad Gorgon University had proven to be nothing but a shell for me. I had been so busy hiding my crystals so that they wouldn't be taken from me, I had hidden all signs of talent. My defensiveness had saved me from becoming an unsuspecting student who might have been forced to study binding spells that could be used against dragons.

Derrick's parents agreed to take in Brittany, Irwin, Teal and Hewitt until we formed a better plan. Or until Hewitt dictated where Teal ended up, no matter what she thought about it.

Lonnie and Star stayed to help lug the tapestry and books to Derrick's cottage. He was going to need a bigger house. Even the cellar was crammed full when we finished.

After carting the last set of books inside, I checked the glen one last time. Lonnie followed and pretended to verify that I had collected the crystals and erased any final signs of the glyphs. When he caught me staring at him, he grinned sheepishly.

"I have to start somewhere," he said. "I can't go back to Central. They'd only put me in the dungeon."

"What did you do?" I asked.

"There was a small mishap."

That statement covered a lot of ground. "Did anyone die this time?"

He shook his head. "Well, no. But there were injuries, and Kal might remain bald unless he gets another wizard to undo it. I'm not sure what went wrong there."

I closed my eyes. "Lonnie..."

"I can learn! I swear! This time if you agree to teach me, I promise I'll study. I will! I have to. The closest school...well, I don't even think I can get into a university. But I'll study this time!"

I waved my hand, dismissing him. "Go with Star. Stay out of trouble. Don't go setting any spells if you can help it."

"He's been well-behaved since I threatened him with the mute spell," Star reported. "He's even taught me a new spell although it didn't work the first time."

Fear coursed through me. "I'd be happy to teach you whatever you want to know." I turned to Lonnie. "Do *not* do any spells without the instructions right in front of you."

"I thought I had the cleaning pots one memorized. But it was missing a symbol."

I looked at Derrick with desperation. He grabbed my hand. I had been pulling on my hair tie only since it had long since fallen out, I was in danger of joining Kal in baldness, one handful at a time.

"Star, ask Zoe next time," Derrick advised.

She smiled. "Come on, cousin Lonnie. Let's go home."

I sighed. Derrick didn't release my hand as we walked back inside. I was unbelievably tired, but there was at least one important task that had to be tackled before sleep. "I need to protect the notes." It was not hard to disguise the notes as something else, but I'd need to figure out how to hide the glyphs from the reveal spell because at least three dragons and one wolf already knew how to make the glyphs glow visibly.

Before long, it was quite possible lots of people would know all about the reveal spell. I shook my head. "Is it good or bad that so many people know magic?"

"Those in Birk know it," Derrick bristled. "Why not us?"

The enormity of the responsibility scared me, but I pulled the gryphon's bundle from under a stack of books and sat at the table. I drew a disguise glyph and used my old white crystal to set it. The gryphon's notes morphed into the appearance of family recipes tied together with a leather thong.

"I wonder what he deemed so important that he kept it hidden," Derrick said.

I clutched his hand in a near panic. Gads. I had disguised one book. There were loads of them. "No one in Birk used a reveal glyph. Of course, even with that, it will take a lot of training to do spells. But it does make it easier to learn how things work. Believe me, being able to see Lonnie's glyphs made my job easier."

I would have released his hand, but he wrapped his larger digits around my fingers and pulled a chair next to me at the table. I leaned against his arm. Using my free hand, I flipped open one of the last books we had brought in. To my surprise, I recognized the text. "Derrick, look!"

"What?"

I tugged my hand. He let go, but scooted closer. I flipped a page. "This is a copy of one of the books from Gorgon's library." I checked the middle and then the glossary. "There's no title on it, but it's one of the books I read a few weeks ago." I reached for another book, but Derrick handed me the one by his hand.

I checked a few pages. "I don't recognize this one specifically, but you know...the style is very similar."

Derrick leaned over and selected two more books from a nearby stack. "Do you think they are all from Gorgon?"

"Could we be so lucky? I assumed everything was burned in the fire."

It took three more tries, but I finally recognized another text. "I've seen this one too. And most of them appear to be typical of the books in the library. Some of them are too advanced for me. The spells are complex or the setup isn't one I recognize, but they are textbooks for sure."

"He must have made personal copies or taken them."

My hand froze in the act of scanning. "That would imply...that he knew the Gorgon books would be lost."

Derrick growled. "It's possible he set the fire himself. Why not? He had what he needed, including a ring to control a dragon. I doubt he intended to live there forever."

I was too tired to consider all the implications. I had showered sometime in the last few hours, but a hot soak in a tub for the next eight hours sounded like heaven. There was no such tub. Derrick caught me eying the pile of blankets.

He turned my head to him. "We need to talk. In the morning."

I nodded a tiny fraction. He leaned in and kissed my lips very gently, and then he let me go, urging me to the blankets with a wave of his hand.

He changed to wolf for his usual check of the perimeter. When he came back in and settled, his glowing eyes were the last thing I saw before deep sleep took me away.

Chapter 22

Derrick snuck out early, leaving me to forage for my own breakfast. Well, not really. He left a generous pitcher of goat's milk and more bread. After two helpings of each, I grabbed my white crystal and my trusty dagger and headed outside.

The birds were slightly more accepting of me, and one of the finches twittered hints of a couple looking for me. "Where?"

Something about trees. Sigh. Well, I knew they weren't perfect messengers.

"Lindis visited this morning," Derrick said from a nearby red oak. I barely jumped. Part of me had adjusted to his tendency to sneak up on me. "When she flew Falk to the roost yesterday, Shae said he delivered your message to your parents."

"Oh good. The finch seemed to have heard something, but it was pretty vague."

"Shae mentioned your parents were delayed in Central or they would have been here by now. It may surprise you to know that cousin Lonnie's name was mentioned in relation to the delay."

I rolled my eyes. "Yes, huge surprise there."

Derrick straightened from where he leaned casually against the tree. "Will you go back with them?"

I found the ground suddenly very interesting and in need of my attention. "What else can I do? I never finished mage school. Only an idiot—or Lonnie—would hire me at this point. I'll need to either find a new school or a new trade."

"Do you want to stay here?"

My eyes flew to his. My throat was too dry to answer him.

He stared at me for a long time, waiting. Wendal was...more than nice, at least with Derrick in it. But Derrick hadn't made me any promises. Or any suggestions, not really. "But I'm not a mage," I squeaked out at last. "I can't just go or stay anywhere I want."

"You have a lot of material to work with, books to keep you busy for a lifetime. And at least one dragon, your cousin and two or three wolves willing to study with you," Derrick said. "Probably Falk too, but he can find a different teacher."

That earned an amused uptick of my lips. Derrick searched my face as though memorizing it.

"The books will definitely be useful to someone," I agreed. The spell books were more valuable than my entire wasted year at Gorgon Uni. Of course, had the mage-master truly been interested in teaching the students, I'd have learned more. Another school might mean better teachers, but I'd have to start all over with entrance exams and getting a scholarship. It might not be possible at all.

Derrick said, "We need someone to study the gryphon notes. Lindis fully intends to involve herself in that chore, but your expertise is worth something to her."

"She has a lot of talent already," I said. "I don't think anyone is going to hire me as a mage. And without that, how will I make a living?"

Now he did smile. "You don't credit yourself enough. You've already taught me and Lindis the basics. You have the books. You learn and then you teach. I won't charge you room and board." He stepped closer, unintentionally or maybe not so unintentionally, stalking me.

My foot would have edged towards him, but the rest of me wasn't willing to assume the risk. "You mean if I teach you?"

Derrick snaked an arm around my waist. "I was thinking of a different exchange. There's a few things I'd like to teach you." He cocked his head. "And I wouldn't mind learning your magic because I seem to be lost underneath it." He leaned in and kissed me softly, giving me time to protest or move away.

I kissed him back, melting under his caress. My hands inched up his chest.

He pulled me closer, brushing his tongue across my mouth just as he had teased my hand days ago. I sucked in a startled breath. Tingles rushed across my skin. It was like being transported; my stomach flipped and my head was no longer connected to the rest of me, but I didn't want to land.

When he gave me the least bit of room to breathe, I opened my mouth to explain the impossibility of it all. "But—" It only encouraged him to kiss me again with even more enthusiasm. He tasted like magic, like all the trees in the forest crashing onto my senses at once.

I went nearly numb with delight. I forgot that I needed to tell him that not everyone would want a silly human half-mage around. I pressed closer, winding my arms around his neck and soaking up the strength in him.

He moved one hand to the back of my neck, brushing back my hair and encouraging me deeper into his kiss.

I was completely safe in the cradle of his arms.

When he finally released me again, he gasped out, "Zoe, will you be my mate? For life?"

My heart couldn't decide whether to beat faster or stop beating completely. It might help if I could just catch my breath. His golden brown eyes held me pinned, the hunger of his kiss secured behind a different kind of need, one that asked for more. "But..." How would I integrate into Wendal? Would I be safe from dungeons? I was nothing but a half-mage! What if...I frowned. "Would you marry me?" I asked. "My parents wouldn't approve if I just stayed here."

He blinked. "Isn't that what I just asked?"

"I don't know. Is it?" My brow furrowed even deeper. "I don't know the vows of Wendal."

A smile cracked across his face as he exploded with a giant burst of laughter. "Well, normally when a man asks a woman for a life commitment, she says yes. Or no. She doesn't usually ask the man the same question. But yes, Zoe. I want to marry you and claim you for my own. Here, there, wherever it's forever."

It was such a large risk. "Really? Are you sure? I am not certain I can bring in much money training anyone in magic. I'm not really a mage, and most of the magic I have learned is quite easy—"

He shut me up with a happy, threatening growl. "I am not marrying you for your talent with spells," he muttered, nuzzling my neck and nipping my jawline. He breathed in deep, as though he could hold the smell of me forever. His hands drifted across my back and bottom, pressing me tightly into the curve of his body.

"Oh." I threw my arms back around his neck and then slowly sank off my tiptoes, reveling in the hard length of him. I had never felt safer and more wanted in my life. "Then yes. I would like to be your life-mate."

He groaned and lifted me up, but then helped me repeat my slide back down. "I'd carry you inside, but only if you promise not to spin me into a tree with one of your crystals."

I dared to nibble his ear. "It depends." I wanted him to kiss me again. And again.

Despite the risk, he picked me up. I kept myself busy wiggling to get more comfortable. He seemed to appreciate my efforts.

The lessons I learned that afternoon were not ones I'd be sharing with any future students. In fact, I was certain I'd need many more before I'd be fully educated.

About the Author

Maria Schneider has published many other novels and short stories:

Under Witch Moon is the first in an urban fantasy series: When dead bodies start turning up Adriel has no choice but to talk to White Feather, an undercover cop. Unfortunately, Adriel is a witch and White Feather isn't convinced she's innocent of wrongdoing. She's going to have to talk fast—and set spells even faster. *Under Witch Aura* is the second in the series.

The Sedona O'Hala series (*Executive Lunch, Executive Retention, Executive Sick Days*) is a series of contemporary cozy mysteries: Sedona must solve a few crimes while fighting her way up the corporate ladder; mostly she dangles from her fingertips, just trying to survive.

Catch an Honest Thief is an adventurous caper across the New Mexico desert; Alexia is in search of treasure, survival and maybe love.

If you're looking for short stories, you might enjoy the anthologies: *Tracking Magic* (Max Killian Investigations), *Sage* (Tales from a Magical Kingdom), *Black-Tie Bingo* or *Year of the Mountain Lion*.

Snitched, Snatched, the original short story that is now the prologue of this novel is still available translated into Spanish.

Maria's website: BearMountainBooks.com